"You are the reason
she's angry with me!"

"I am?" Miguel said, gripping her arms.
"Tell me the rest, Kirstie."

It was embarrassing to have to tell him
the cause of Rosa's jealousy. "It wasn't...
I mean she saw you kiss me. I realize it
wasn't anything important to you," she
declared, "but Señora Montanes took a
different view, considering her...
personal interest."

Miguel eyed her narrowly. "Personal
interest?" he asked ominously.

"She considers you private property,"
Kirstie snapped. "And if Luis hadn't told
me, I'd have had proof enough just
now!"

"Rosa's behavior proves nothing except
her dislike of a younger and prettier
woman," Miguel argued harshly. "And
Luis should have better things to do than
discuss me—or anybody in the family—
with you!"

"The hired help!" Kirstie
observed bitterly.

REBECCA STRATTON
is also the author of these
Harlequin Romances

and these
Harlequin Presents

Many of these titles are available at your local bookseller.

For a free catalogue listing all available Harlequin Romances
and Harlequin Presents, send your name and address to:

HARLEQUIN READER SERVICE
1440 South Priest Drive, Tempe, AZ 85281
Canadian address: Stratford, Ontario N5A 6W2

The Black Invader

by

REBECCA STRATTON

Harlequin Books

TORONTO · LONDON · LOS ANGELES · AMSTERDAM
SYDNEY · HAMBURG · PARIS · STOCKHOLM · ATHENS · TOKYO

Original hardcover edition published in 1981
by Mills & Boon Limited

ISBN 0-373-02452-5

Harlequin edition published January 1982

CHAPTER ONE

KIRSTIE was already half-turned in the saddle before last-minute recognition of the voice pulled her up short, her back stiff and straight and resentment in every line of her slender body. It showed too in her deep blue eyes as she held her head high so that the light breeze of her own making lifted the black hair from her neck and tossed it back into a wild mane. There was an almost primitive beauty about her, and an unmistakable air of pride that came from generations of noble forebears.

The neat little mare she rode would have extended a warmer welcome to the advancing newcomers, recognising a stablemate, but her rider held her too firmly in check with tightly clenched hands. Hands that clenched even more tightly when the attempt to attract her attention was repeated.

'Señorita Rodríguez!'

Kirstie could hardly ignore it altogether, but she could and did refuse to offer encouragement by turning her head, for she had no doubt at all who it was riding up on her, or that Miguel Montañes was about to join her, whether or not he was encouraged. She would rather it was anyone but him, no matter if her grandfather did accuse her of being not only unsociable but downright rude.

When he rode up alongside her Kirstie sneaked a sidelong look at him from the concealment of her lashes, and she was forced to admit, however grudgingly, that she had never seen a man sit a horse with more confidence and ease, or look more impressive. The way he handled the big Arab stallion he rode was merely an extension of the same arrogance that was one of the reasons for Kirstie's dislike of him, and she noted how the big creature responded obediently to the hard pressure of muscular legs.

He was too confident, too arrogant in his superiority, yet he always somehow managed to convey the impression that he found her resentment of him regrettable but understandable in the circumstances, and his tolerance added to her dislike of him. He was smiling faintly, she noticed, an imperturbable and slightly cynical smile that always angered her.

According to her grandfather, who seemed to have a penchant for collecting information, the Montañes had come originally from Andalucia, and were descended from the Moors who had occupied Spain for so many hundreds of years, something that Kirstie found easy enough to believe when she looked at Miguel Montañes. He had a swarthiness that was much darker than her grandfather's complexion, and a certain hawkishness in the cast of his features that made the story only too likely to be true.

Dark Spanish eyes regarded her steadily, but it was difficult to assess their expression, and the strong, dark-skinned features gave nothing away. 'May I ride with you, *señorita*?'

Kirstie would much rather he did not ride with her, for she found him much too discomforting because of the tolerance with which he treated her obvious dislike of him. A harsh and uncompromising lack of understanding would have been easier to deal with, but he seemed to realise exactly how she felt about losing the Casa de Rodríguez and, what was worse, pitied her.

'I'm not even sure which way I'm going,' she told him, being as discouraging as possible. 'I'm simply riding, Señor Montañes, and I'm not in any particular hurry either.'

It was an abrupt and extremely discourteous response and one that would have appalled her grandfather, but somehow Kirstie always found it impossible to respond to this man as she did to other people. She recalled the number of times during the past month when she had seen him riding across the *huerta*, as if he and his mount responded as one to some irresistible call. But not for anything would she have him know that the sight of them in the distance always filled her with a strange and disturbing sense of excitement.

'I'm not in any particular hurry either,' he assured her gravely, and because he accepted her ungraciousness without visible resentment, she coloured furiously.

His deep and, she had to admit, rather pleasant voice always seemed to assume a slightly pedantic tone whenever he spoke to her, and Kirstie suspected it might be because, despite nearly seven years in Spain, her Spanish was still faintly accented. She knew too that her grandfather had confided in him; told him how she came to live in Spain when her widowed Scottish mother remarried and that she was his only grandchild. In fact his easy and immediate friendship with her grandfather was another point against him in Kirstie's eyes, for she felt that her one comforter in the loss of the Casa de Rodríguez was less in sympathy with her because of it.

'I would still like to accompany you,' Miguel Montañes told her, 'with your permission, *señorita*.'

'You may go wherever you like on your own property, Señor Montañes,' she told him with a bitterness she could not disguise, and he made no reply for a moment.

The glance he gave her unfriendly face spoke volumes, however, and yet again Kirstie felt her colour rise. He rode alongside her, holding the powerful stallion to a pace more suited to her own smaller mount, and she carefully kept her gaze straight ahead and her chin angled discouragingly. If she was quite honest with herself, she would have admitted that her intense dislike of him stemmed originally from the fact that he had been the one who actually negotiated the purchase of the Casa de Rodríguez, although he was not the sole owner. She would have felt precisely the same about anyone who took possession of the house and lands that had been in her family for more than two hundred years.

'You dislike me intensely don't you, Señorita Rodríguez?'

The question broke into her musing, and she turned her head instinctively, a sweep of long lashes quickly concealing the surprise she showed. Such bluntness was unexpected, and she felt it left her more vulnerable. 'Don't you think I have reason to?' she challenged defensively, and his reply was swift and just as abrasive as his original question had been.

'No, *señorita*, I do not!'

Feeling at too much of a disadvantage to follow it up, Kirstie was silent. Although he was so much older than she was, in other circumstances she was prepared to allow that she would have recognised him as a very attractive man, despite his arrogance. As it was he stood very little chance of even being liked, and only very occasionally did a small twinge of conscience tell her that she was being unreasonable. When it stirred it was at once suppressed.

In the early years of her life she had known many happy times at Casa de Rodríguez; when her time had been divided between her Spanish father's family home and her mother's country, and the years after her father's death had perhaps lent a dreamlike quality to its memory. But she had lived with her grandfather for more than six years now, and in that time she had developed a fierce and possessive love for the place, so that she hated the very idea of it passing into other hands.

She had wept bitterly when her grandfather told her that a disastrous business venture had ruined him, and that the house and lands would have to be sacrificed to provide enough for him to live on. The option had been quickly taken up by the Montañes and so, with a few remnants of furniture and the bare necessities of life, the two of them had moved into a tiny, whitewashed *barraca* that had once housed their overseer.

It was within sight of the house, at the far end of a tree-shaded ride, and that was almost worse than moving completely away, Kirstie sometimes felt, for it was a constant reminder of all that the once proud and prolific Rodríguez had lost. They were now reduced to one old man and a twenty-year-old girl, living in a *barraca* on the estate, and that was a very bitter pill to swallow.

It had been Miguel Montañes who took the unexpected step of allowing Kirstie and her grandfather the freedom of the estate, and suggested that she might still care to ride the gentle mare she was so attached to but could not possibly take with her. It was an oddly disarming gesture that she would rather he had not made, except that she could not resist the chance to take out the pretty, golden-coated mare sometimes.

But it was her grandfather's seemingly passive acceptance of their situation that she found most difficult to come to terms with, for he had settled into the tiny cottage with far less complaints than she had herself, and sometimes made her feel rather ashamed. Even one servant was out of the question, so that Kirstie had needed to call upon the domestic skills that her practical Scottish mother had insisted she learned, and very occasionally it surprised her to realise that she actually enjoyed cooking meals for them.

One thing was still available to her; the vista of the *huerta* with its fertile acres of oranges and olives, and dotted with little white *barracas* just like the one she lived in with her grandfather. Most of the vast fertile plain was divided into smallholdings, subdivided by the precious irrigation system, and the Casa de Rodríguez lands were one of the very few large estates left. There was nowhere in the world to compare with the *huerta* of Valencia, and she loved it.

As if by silent consent they reined to a halt where the olives ended and the orange trees began, and the scent of them drifted over them with the light breeze. Sensing an air of preoccupation, Kirstie glanced at the man beside her and frowned curiously, for she could not believe that her dislike of him disturbed him to any degree.

'Are you settling down in your new home?' he asked,

and Kirstie looked at him sharply, suspecting something more than the obvious behind the question.

'I suppose so,' she replied cautiously. 'It isn't easy to adjust, but——' She shrugged, leaving the rest of the sentence unsaid.

'Don José appears to have adapted well,' he observed. 'He tells me that he's quite comfortable.'

Kirstie looked at him and her blue eyes were darkly shadowed. 'What else do you expect him to say?' she asked bitterly. 'He's a proud man and he's making the best of the situation because he knows he hasn't much choice.'

'While you are equally determined *not* to make the best of the situation,' Miguel Montañes suggested, and met her resentful gaze steadily. 'You have no intention of making the best of something you can do nothing to alter, have you, Señorita Rodríguez? You will not accept that things could not go on as they were but must change drastically whether or not you like it.'

It was a discomfitingly shrewd observation that Kirstie had to admit was true, although she had no intention of letting him know it. 'The Casa de Rodríguez is—was my home,' she reminded him in a voice that shivered with emotion. 'It's been in my family for more than two hundred years, and one doesn't give up a heritage like that easily, Señor Montañes. How can you know how it feels to lose everything your family has possessed for so long?'

'I know it very well, *señorita*.' His quietness impressed her yet again with the sincerity of his feelings for her situation, but it did nothing to soften her attitude towards him. Miguel Montañes was not the type of man who invited sympathy. 'Although it was before I was born, my family suffered the same kind of loss in the years before the war that tore our country in two. We know the bitterness of losing everything, we knew it for almost fifty years, but self-pity is not a constructive emotion, and obviously Don José has the intelligence to accept things as they are. He retains his dignity and pride even though he has lost everything else.'

'He has no choice but to accept!' Kirstie retorted sharply, for she couldn't fail to recognise that he was laying the blame for her present bitter unhappiness at her own door.

'But he accepts it,' he insisted. 'Wisdom comes with age, so they say, and as it's necessary for you to live in a *barraca,* your grandfather has enough wisdom to make the best of what cannot be changed. Why don't you do the same, Señorita Rodríguez?'

She looked at him for several moments, trying to imagine how this man's family had come to terms with their similar loss, and knowing that it was because of it that he was so tolerant of her bitterness. 'Oh, you just don't understand,' she told him despairingly at last.

'Of course I understand,' he told her quietly. 'What I don't understand is your almost psychopathic hatred of me merely because I was the one who negotiated the purchase of the estate. It simply isn't reasonable.'

'You—you don't understand,' she said again, and kept her face averted because she knew in her heart that he did understand, and the realisation was disturbing.

The stallion shifted restlessly and hard brown hands brought him swiftly under control with the minimum of effort. 'Please believe that I know exactly how you feel,' Miguel Montañes assured her. 'But it requires a great deal of money to maintain a place like this, you must realise that, and Don José no longer has the means. He's refreshingly frank about his mistakes, and one has to admire him for it—personally I find him an admirable man in every way.'

'He is.' Her bottom lip was trembling so that Kirstie bit on it hastily before he realised how near to tears he brought her by his opinion of her grandfather.

She looked a strange and beautiful mixture of child and woman with her dishevelled black hair and the shining dark threat of tears in her blue eyes, and Miguel Montañes watched her for a moment with a warmth in his eyes for the wild, gamin beauty of her. Then he shook his head slowly.

What he would have said, Kirstie neither cared nor
waited to find out, but urged her animal forward with a
light dig of her heels. The mare responded willingly and
Kirstie gave her her head for a moment, enjoying the
movement and the breeze created by it, and heedless of
whether or not Miguel Montañes chose to follow.

'Señorita Rodríguez!'

She ignored the call, using the distance between them
as an excuse for not having heard, but the distance was
soon lessened and the big stallion came thundering up
behind them, making the mare waywardly skittish and
harder to handle. Kirstie could handle her, but control
was taken out of her hands when Miguel Montañes
reached over and took the bridle, pulling both animals
to a halt.

Kirstie was breathing rapidly, as if she and not her
horse had been running, and she cast a swift look from
the corner of her eye at the face of the man beside her.
His mouth had a hard set look that cautioned discretion,
but she was feeling strangely lightheaded, and not in the
mood to be cautious, so that she looked at him down
the length of her small nose and showed a warning glint
in her eyes.

'Please don't do that!' she objected, but the long
brown fingers remained firmly hooked into the bridle
and held the mare close alongside, a situation that
neither Kirstie nor her mount were happy with.

'I have something I wish to say to you,' he informed
her, 'and since you seem determined not to let me have
my say, *señorita*, I am obliged to use force to bring you
into line.'

His arrogance was staggering and Kirstie's colour was
high as she hung on tightly to the skittering mare, but
there was very little she could do about moving out of
his reach. 'I hope it's something important, *señor*,' she
told him shortly. 'I'm not in the habit of being *forced* to
listen to anyone, nor am I accustomed to being—
brought into line!'

'It appears to me,' Miguel Montañes retorted equally sharply, 'that you're not in the habit of doing anything except exactly what *you* like, *señorita*, regardless of the feelings of others or how bad-mannered you appear! No wonder you embarrass your grandfather!'

Furious at being reprimanded like an ill-bred child, Kirstie snatched the bridle free and jabbed hard into the mare's flanks, so that the animal took off like the wind, leaving the stallion and his rider standing. Not for long, however, for the bigger animal took off suddenly and the chase was on; a chase that was none of her choosing, Kirstie told herself as she gave the mare her head.

Not for a moment did it occur to her that she had absolutely no excuse for behaving as she was, but the desire to outrun him was irresistible, and there was an undeniable thrill in the chase that stirred her blood unexpectedly. All too soon the stallion raced up alongside, and when she glanced from the corner of her eye the expression she saw on her pursuer's face sent a rippling shiver along her spine.

He made no attempt to stop her this time, but kept alongside, holding the stronger stallion to her pace and watching her with swift dark looks that promised there was no escape. The mare's ears were pricked and she knew herself to be outclassed if it came to a challenge, but she kept gamely on until Kirstie recognised the inevitability of it and eventually allowed the pace to slacken, finally coming to a halt.

Immediately Miguel Montañes did the same, and with both animals breathing hard they stood for a moment, unspeaking. Then he dismounted and tethered his horse to a tree before coming round to the other side of the mare. He stood looking up at Kirstie for a second, then reached up and grasped her around the waist, hauling her bodily out of the saddle and setting her firmly down on her feet.

'Perhaps now I may have your attention, *señorita*,' he said and, in case she might have it in mind to remount and ride off, he took the reins from her and flung them over a branch.

Kirstie's heart was thudding wildly, for she had never seen him in this mood before. He was always autocratic, and he was tolerant to the point of being infuriating, but she had never experienced this curious air of menacing excitement before. It affected her in a way she did not understand, and at the same time made her quite certain that he would have his say, whatever it was, and whether or not she wanted to hear it.

Her hands were clasped together in front of her and she did not look up, even though she felt him watching her still. 'I hope after the effort you went to that this proves important, Señor Montañes,' she told him in a slightly unsteady voice.

'Don José seemed to think it would be of some importance to you,' he said, and Kirstie looked up swiftly at the mention of her grandfather. 'He tells me that you're looking for work, *señorita*, is that right?'

Kirstie eyed him furiously. She hated having it put into such flat, down-to-earth terms, however true it was, and she couldn't bring herself to accept the idea of her grandfather discussing it with this man of all people. 'I didn't expect my grandfather to discuss my private affairs with a stranger,' she told him, her eyes brightly angry. 'I trusted him and he shouldn't have told you!'

'And you shouldn't speak of your grandfather in that tone!' Miguel Montañes told her sharply. 'What Don José discusses with me is his affair; you are his granddaughter and he has every right to talk about you if he wishes to. As it happens it came up in the normal course of conversation, and there was no indiscretion involved.' His eyes gleamed blackly at her and she had never seen those stern features look so menacing before. 'Mother of God, child, do you suspect everyone of wishing you harm?'

'Not everyone, no!'

His eyes narrowed as he looked down at her, and Kirstie fumed at his reference to her as 'child'. It was that as much as anything that made her act as she did. Turning her back on him, she reached for the mare's rein, but before she could loose it a hand on her wrist swung her round again so forcefully that she almost lost her balance. The same hands steadied her against falling, and for a moment the heat of his palms burned through her thin shirt into her flesh, so that she caught her breath.

'Don't turn your back on me, my girl!' he ordered harshly. 'Why I'm concerning myself with you after the way you've behaved, heaven alone knows, but I promised Don José I'd have a word with you and you're going to listen to me even if I have to hold you forcibly while I talk!'

'You——'

'Listen, damn you!' He shook her hard, glaring relentlessly into her flushed and angry face, but his words penetrated simply because of their sheer unexpectedness. 'You took secretarial training in your last two years at school, I understand?' Kirstie nodded automatically. 'Don José claims you were very good, and by coincidence my uncle is in need of a secretary. Whether or not the two needs can be satisfied at one stroke depends very much on you, Señorita Rodríguez. Your Spanish is almost faultless, and providing you come up to standard in other respects and can learn to control that childish resentment, I see no reason why you shouldn't be suitable.'

The look in her eyes betrayed how stunned she was, and Kirstie tried desperately to get things into perspective. 'But I don't know——' she began.

'You would be working at the Casa de Rodríguez,' he went on. 'I imagine that would be an added attraction.'

Surprise followed surprise and Kirstie stared at him. 'At the house?'

He nodded, but she was unaware of a certain look in his eyes that recognised the first sign of weakening. 'If you're interested and can stop behaving like a spoiled child, come and see my uncle this afternoon for an interview.'

'I—I don't think I've ever seen him.'

It had only just occurred to her that as members of the same family, he and his uncle could be expected to share some family characteristics, and Miguel Montañes was not the kind of employer she had in mind when she spoke of taking a job. Evidently something of the sort had crossed his mind too, for a faint smile touched his mouth for just a moment.

'If you're concerned in case my uncle is anything like me, or I am like him,' he told her, 'you have no need to worry.' Kirstie hastily dropped her eyes, uneasy at being so accurately read. 'You really do dislike me, don't you, Señorita Rodríguez?'

Kirstie shifted her uneasy gaze about the landscape of trees and rice-fields and little white *barracas*, and wished he wouldn't watch her so intently. 'I don't see that you can blame me for that,' she said.

'But I do!'

The violence of his response startled her so that she turned her head involuntarily to look at him. He had a strong, almost harsh profile and he carried his head with the pride of a Moorish lord from whom, according to her grandfather, he was descended. Everything about him suggested power, and not least the hawkish features, tanned and weathered by the sun, and the almost black, thick-fringed eyes that watched her so steadily.

His proximity was oddly affecting, and it was the reason she apologised without really knowing why she did it, and in a strangely breathless voice. 'I'm sorry.'

When he raised a hand just briefly to run it through his hair, his arm brushed hers and sent unexpected shivers through her, and his anger seemed suddenly to have cooled with her apology. 'I'd like to believe that,' he said quietly. 'Shall I make an appointment for you to see my uncle this afternoon?' Kirstie nodded, taken aback to realise it was to be so soon. 'Will about three-thirty suit you?'

Again she nodded, bringing herself hastily back to earth when she realised that something a little more definite was required of her. 'Yes, that will be fine, thank you.' She moistened her lips anxiously. 'Shall I come to the house?'

'Naturally.' She gasped when a long finger slid beneath her chin and raised her face so that he looked directly down into it. 'You won't mind too much?' he asked, and softness edged his voice and showed in his eyes, as if he knew exactly how she would feel going back.

'I'll mind,' she whispered, 'but I'll come.'

'Good!'

Again Kirstie turned to loose the mare's rein, but again she was prevented from achieving it by a hand on her arm. This time, however, it was a much less forceful touch and when she turned towards him she did so quite voluntarily, meeting his eyes for a moment, and then quickly lowering them to his mouth, although it was hardly less disturbing.

Her pulse was thudding rapidly and her legs felt strangely unsteady, yet she found it hard to attribute the way she felt entirely to the proximity of Miguel Montañes. There was no shred of doubt about his masculinity, but she had never before been quite so stunningly aware of it as now, when he stood close enough for their bodies to just lightly touch. It was an inescapable contact because the mare was pressed against her back, and one shattering to her self-control, but there was nothing she could do about it.

The mare shifted restlessly and nudged her still closer and his hands curved about her upper arms, holding her for a moment to the pulsing warmth of his body, while he looked down into her face with an intensity she found unnerving. 'I hope I haven't made a mistake by suggesting you have this job,' he said in a curiously rough voice, and Kirstie caught her breath when a long forefinger lifted a wisp of hair from her neck briefly before letting it flutter back. 'You're very young and so determinedly—touchy I wonder if you'll do after all.'

'You can't change your mind now!' she objected,

anxious, now that there was a chance of losing it, to have the job with his uncle.

Miguel Montañes studied her for a moment longer, then shook his head, letting his hands drop to his sides. 'No, I can't,' he agreed, and reached to untether her horse. 'Are you ready to ride back?' he asked, and was waiting to help her mount, Kirstie realised, if she agreed.

'Not yet—thank you.'

Her response was instinctive and for a moment he regarded her steadily, then he shrugged his broad shoulders resignedly and turned to fetch his own horse. 'Of course,' he said, as if he understood her reluctance.

Kirstie watched him mount and when he eventually sat, tall and impressive in the saddle again, she realised for the first time that her attitude towards him, her wary suspicion, did not entirely stem from his having been the one to negotiate the purchase of Casa de Rodríguez. It was something about the man himself; an aura of menacing virility that was frankly disturbing.

Pulling the stallion round where he could look directly down into her face, he held her eyes for a moment. 'Don't be nervous of meeting my uncle, Señorita Rodríguez,' he told her, 'we're not alike.' Briefly she glimpsed that faintly cynical smile again as he turned away. 'You'll *like* him!'

He jabbed hard with his heels and applied the quirt to the stallion's rump, and the animal sprang forward eagerly, taking the way between the ranks of twisted olive trees at a speed that raised little spurts of dust in his wake. Miguel did not turn his head, but very briefly the quirt was raised in a gesture of farewell, and Kirstie watched him go with dark, thoughtful eyes.

There would be advantages to working at Casa de Rodríguez, she could not deny it. For one thing it would entail no travelling getting to work, since it was literally on her doorstep, but there could be disadvantages too. If the uncle she was to work for proved to be more like him than Miguel Montañes said, it wouldn't be easy working for him, and then there was the question of whether his two brothers resembled him as well. Nor was she quite sure how she would feel about walking into her old home every day as a stranger with no voice in the running of it. Turning to remount her horse, she sighed as she swung upward. She could only hope that she wasn't getting into something that she couldn't cope with.

It was the first time that Kirstie had been required to earn her living, and the prospect of her first interview filled her with misgivings as the time approached. It had nothing to do with not being fully qualified, for she had passed all her tests at school with flying colours, but rather the fact that the man who was to interview her was a Montañes; someone she was going to find it hard not to see as an interloper.

She thought her grandfather regarded her rather anxiously as she took a last look at herself, and she swung her black hair in a gesture that could have been interpreted as defiance. José Rodríguez was seventy years old and had spent the whole of his life, until the past few months, surrounded by the ease and luxury that his birth and upbringing had accustomed him to. Only now did Kirstie begin to realise how much harder it was for him than for herself, and her decision to ease their financial situation by working, she realised, was a practical way of helping him.

He was a man of medium height whose carriage and posture gave the impression that he was much taller, and all the qualities of the old nobility were embodied in him. His hair was iron grey with scarcely any of its raven blackness still evident, and his eyes were dark and steady, showing only a trace of the sadness that had aged him several years in the past few months.

Turning from the mirror, Kirstie grasped his arms and kissed him on both cheeks. 'Don't worry, Abuelo,' she whispered, 'I'll behave very properly, so that you won't be ashamed of me. I promise.'

Don José smiled gently, his long fingers touching her cheek. 'I shall never be ashamed of you, child,' he promised. 'And I'm certain Señor Montañes will give you the job; his nephew seemed confident that he would.'

'Then he won't dare do anything else!' Kirstie remarked pertly, and immediately pulled a face. 'I'm sorry, Abuelo, but just as long as I don't need to come into contact with Miguel Montañes I might be able to cope.' She kissed him again lightly and smiled. 'Goodbye!'

Don José watched from the window as she walked with a deceptively confident step along the familiar tree-lined ride through the orange grove, but he couldn't see the suspicious brightness in her eyes as she approached her old home, only the slim straightness of her back and the proud lift of her head. Ever since they had been forced to leave the Casa de Rodríguez she had promised herself that she would come back one day, but she had never imagined it would be as an employee of the new owners, and the resentment she felt still stuck like an immovable bone in her throat.

At the end of the ride a tall arched gateway with a wrought iron gate gave access to the gardens, and there was a heart-aching familiarity about it all that quickened Kirstie's pulse. When she pushed open the gate the walled *patio* gardens spilled colour and scent into the hot air, cooled only where a fringe of citrus trees grew against the surrounding walls. Roses, carnations and deep red oleanders crowded the wide beds, and urns filled with musky bright geraniums splashed their colour over the tiled entrance formed by an overhanging balcony running the width of the house and draped with vines of bougainvillea, morning glory and yellow roses.

It seemed that nothing at all had changed, and for a moment Kirstie stood amid the colourful profusion and tried to pretend that all was as it had been before. Her eyes were bright with emotion and a hard lump in her throat refused to be swallowed no matter how hard she tried. Then the big blackwood door opened and Miguel

Montañes stood in the opening for a moment watching her, before he spoke.

'Señorita Rodríguez—will you come in?'

Kirstie swallowed her pride. It wasn't easy to accept an invitation to enter what had been her own home, as if she was a stranger to it, but she nodded her thanks and for the first time in just over a month walked into the cool elegance of Casa de Rodríguez.

It surprised her to realise how few changes had been made in fact. There were one or two different pieces of furniture in the hall, and the old ivory crucifix that had been in the Rodríguez family for more than a hundred years had been replaced by a bigger and more ornate bronze one. But the same small table stood below it, displaying a vase of white carnations from the garden, just as it had always done.

The white walls still contrasted with black beams and a highly polished block floor, and incredibly one or two of the same paintings glowed richly in the shadowed coolness between arched doorways. It was a shock to realise that the Rodríguez family portraits that had taken pride of place, but could not be found room in their new accommodation, had been displaced by what were evidently portraits of past Montañes, and she wondered what had happened to her own forebears.

'They're safely stored, not sold or destroyed, you have my word.'

Kirstie looked at him in momentary confusion, then realised that he was referring to the missing portraits and gave him a faint, uneasy smile. 'I'm glad,' she said huskily. 'Thank you.'

He nodded, as if yet again he understood exactly how she was feeling, then extended one hand in invitation. 'Will you come this way? My uncle is waiting for you.'

He led the way across the hall to what had once been a small and seldom used *salón*, but which was now completely converted for business use. Unlike the hall it retained none of its original furnishings, although a particularly exquisite landscape that she had always liked still adorned the wall above the fireplace.

A huge desk occupied the space immediately in front of the fireplace and another, smaller one stood over beside the window, while steel filing cabinets lined the walls and gave the room a stark, businesslike air. When Miguel Montañes opened the door a man seated at the larger of the two desks looked up immediately and smiled, but remained seated, and it was not until she shook hands with him that Kirstie realised Enrique Montañes was confined to a wheelchair.

He was, she guessed, about fifty-three or four years old and bore quite a strong physical resemblance to his autocratic nephew, although his hair was greying brown rather than that raven-black and he seemed much less arrogant. There were sharp lines etched at the corners of his mouth that ran deep furrows upward beside an aristocratic nose, so that Kirstie could guess he suffered a great deal of pain. It was not only sympathy, however, that made her decide that she liked him just as instinctively as she had disliked the younger man, and at that moment she saw nothing illogical in it.

'Please sit down, Señorita Rodriguez,' he told her with a smile. 'I'm so glad you decided to come and see me.'

Instinctively Kirstie glanced over her shoulder before she took the chair he offered, and found Miguel at her shoulder, waiting to help her to her seat. He leaned over her, pushing the chair against the backs of her knees, and she sat down automatically, murmuring her thanks as she did so and very conscious of his physical presence and of the light brush of his hands on her shoulders for a moment when he drew back.

'I understand you trained in secretarial work,' said Enrique Montañes, obviously seeking to put her at her ease. 'Is that the extent of your experience, *señorita*?'

'I'm afraid so,' Kirstie confessed. 'I've never actually worked at it; I hope you don't think I came here hoping for——' She bit back the suggestion she had been about to make, and decided that for all his seeming kindliness Enrique Montañes was unlikely to give anyone a job as secretary out of charity. 'I realise you probably want someone more experienced,' she amended, and he smiled at her reassuringly.

'Everyone has to begin somewhere, Señorita Rodríguez, and if your typing and shorthand speeds are up to my requirements then I see no reason why you shouldn't get your experience here. Do you have your diplomas with you?'

'Oh yes, of course.' She foraged in her handbag for a moment and produced the required certificates, explaining as she handed them over, 'I was top in class each term, and if I've lost a little speed I'm sure I could soon pick it up again.'

'I'm sure you could,' Enrique concurred as he flipped through the papers, and he was smiling when he handed them back to her. 'You appear to have earned your position as top in class, Señorita Rodríguez, but in fact your typing is of more importance to me because I'm one of those curious people who find it difficult to think as I dictate.' He laughed at his own shortcomings and used his hands to dismiss any need to apologise for them. 'Do you think you will be able to cope with such an inefficient employer?'

'I'm willing to try,' Kirstie assured him. 'But I think I ought to stress, Señor Montañes, that I've done neither shorthand nor typing since I left school.'

'Which surely cannot be so very long ago,' he guessed with a smile. 'You're very young, my dear *señorita*.'

Miguel Montañes was sitting with arrogant ease on the end of the second desk, and it was instinctive when she glanced over her shoulder at him before she answered, meeting for a moment his steady and disconcerting gaze. 'I'm twenty,' she said, and wondered why it should sound more as if she challenged that bright, dark gaze than merely answered a simple question. 'I shall be twenty-one in three months' time, but I hope you don't feel I'm too young to cope, Señor Montañes.'

'Not at all,' he assured her. But from the way he sat studying the tips of his fingers Kirstie suspected there was something else on his mind. 'There is perhaps the question of your feelings regarding the Casa de Rodríguez, *señorita*. I understand that you feel a certain— resentment at the loss of your home, which is quite understandable in the circumstances, but it might not prove an ideal situation were you employed by us.'

It wasn't a situation that Kirstie was sure she could explain very well, especially with Miguel Montañes sitting close by and watching her with that steady, disturbing gaze of his. If it had been a case of working for him she would not even have considered it, but she thought she could work for his uncle without her emotions getting the better of her, and it occurred to her for the first time that she had better make sure that Enrique Montañes was to have exclusive claim to her services.

'I would be working for *you*, wouldn't I, Señor Montañes?' she asked, and noticed the way he looked quickly in his nephew's direction before he replied.

'For the most part, *señorita*, yes.'

'Señorita Rodríguez merely wishes to be sure that she will not be called upon to work for me, that's all, Tío Enrique.' Miguel's smooth deep voice forestalled her reply, and Kirstie coloured furiously at being so precisely interpreted yet again.

'Is that right, *señorita*?'

Both men were watching her with such intentness that she found it embarrassing, and she looked down at the hands in her lap because she did not know what to say. Heaven knew why Miguel Montañes was still there, but his presence made it impossible for her to appear at her best, and she did not see how she could deny her reluctance to work for him when he at least must be perfectly well aware of it.

'That's right, *señor*,' she agreed in a huskily unsteady voice. 'I—I couldn't work for Señor Montañes.'

'I see.'

She quite expected that Miguel would condemn her for her prejudice, but for the moment he was saying nothing, he merely lingered there in the background as if he waited to see what the eventual outcome would be. On the other hand her insistence obviously troubled the older man, for he was frowning uneasily, and tapping the fingers of one hand on his desk.

'I don't know, Señorita Rodríguez,' he said. 'Perhaps in view of your strong feelings we should reconsider the advisability of employing you.'

Kirstie heard him with dismay, and none the less so because she realised how much she had contributed to the decision, by taking such an obvious stand against having anything to do with Miguel Montañes. She sat for a moment with her hands clasped tightly on her lap and tried to think of a way to escape without letting them see just how disappointed she was.

In the event she had no time to think of anything before Miguel came across to his uncle's desk with long, impatient strides and rested one hand on the edge of it while the other was used to emphasise what he was saying. Leaning down so that his face was close to hers, he spoke to Kirstie with the same brusque impatience he had shown so often before.

'Don't be a little fool,' he told her shortly. 'Why lose an opportunity like this simply because you can't resist showing your dislike of me? If it concerns you to such an extent, I'll guarantee that you won't see any more of me than is absolutely necessary; there's little reason why we should meet anyway in the normal course of things. In the name of heaven, child, be sensible!'

Kirstie's colour was high as she glared into the dark face so close that she could see the fine lines at the corners of his eyes, and it was debatable that what she said would have improved matters at all. In the event it was Enrique Montañes who took a hand. 'Miguel, there's no reason for you to make such a promise—if Señorita Rodríguez doesn't feel she can fit in, then it's best that she doesn't take the job.'

'She can fit in,' Miguel insisted stubbornly. Straightening up, he ran a hand through his thick black hair and looked down at Kirstie in a way that challenged her to deny what he was saying. 'She's capable of doing the work and she wants the job, so why in heaven's name all this quibbling? I spend so little time here, at least during the hours Señorita Rodríguez will be here, that it doesn't really matter; settle it now so that she can begin in the morning and you can get some of that backlog of work cleared that's been worrying you for so long.'

There was obviously still some doubt in the older man's mind, but the forceful argument put forward by his nephew was bound to have an effect, and Kirstie doubted if anyone bothered denying him for very long. She hadn't said another word, either in her own defence, or in agreement with his very logical argument, but she waited anxiously while Enrique Montañes made up his mind.

'The situation is rather desperate, Señorita Rodríguez,' he admitted. 'Do you feel you could be happy here in the circumstances?'

Kirstie was sure she could, even allowing for an occasional encounter with Miguel Montañes, and she was almost eager now to take the job. 'I'm sure I could, señor,' she assured him, trying to ignore the disturbing proximity of his nephew. 'And——' she glanced briefly up at the face that still seemed to hover over her even now he was standing upright, 'I'm sorry I spoke so hastily.'

For a moment Enrique Montañes' gaze switched rapidly from Kirstie's flushed face to his nephew's dark and broodingly implacable one, then he smiled faintly and shook his head. 'You're very young and very— impulsive, I think, my dear señorita,' he said. 'But if you would like to work for us—for me, will you please be here by nine o'clock tomorrow morning? Can you manage that?'

Kirstie hastily came to terms with the fact that her working life was to begin almost immediately, and she took a moment or two to adjust to the idea while the two men watched her closely. Looking across the desk, she gave Enrique Montañes a faint but definite smile and nodded. 'I can manage that, *señor*,' she said. 'Thank you.'

'Then I shall see you in the morning.' A kindly smile encouraged her as she got to her feet, and she grasped the hand he proffered a little dazedly. 'I'm sure we shall we get along together very well, my dear *señorita. Adios!*'

She was shaking like a leaf, she realised as she walked across the room, and it was a moment or two before she registered the fact that Miguel Montañes had accompanied her out of the room and was walking out into the garden with her. It was as they crossed the cool, tiled verandah that she turned and looked up at him, and surprised a faint smile on that usually stern face.

'You like my uncle?' he asked, and Kirstie had no need to think before she answered.

'Very much; I shall like working for him.'

'And yet you almost put an end to the whole thing by making your dislike of me so obvious that even Tío Enrique couldn't overlook it!' He came with her as she followed the path to the gateway, and she wondered why he was bothering, in view of her behaviour a few minutes ago. 'We're nothing alike, you see,' he remarked, and it was a second or two before Kirstie remembered the promise he had made to that effect.

When she answered as she did it was a deliberate misunderstanding and she pursed her lips in consideration. 'Oh, I don't know, I think you look quite a lot alike.'

'Not so alike as we once were,' Miguel remarked, and something in his voice made her look up again so that she noticed a tightness about his mouth, and a kind of drawn look that suggested feelings held firmly under control. 'Three years ago my uncle's legs were shattered in a car crash. It was the same crash that killed both my parents and my cousin Juan, his son, but I sometimes think that for an active man such as my uncle was, being crippled for life is an almost greater tragedy.'

It was the closest she had yet come to the private

man, and Kirstie felt touched in a way she had never
expected to be by him. It was a curiously disturbing
experience, and when she replied it was in a small and
somewhat husky voice. 'I'm very sorry,' she said. 'I had
no idea.'

'Of course you hadn't.' He said no more for a moment
and Kirstie suspected it was a subject he didn't often
mention. Why he had seen fit to tell her she could not
imagine, but she began to suspect that he was a man
who was full of surprises. It was also unexpected to
realise that the silence between them as they walked
through the gardens was an oddly companionable one.
'You're a very small family, aren't you?' he asked after
a moment or two. 'Just you and your grandfather, I
understand.'

Matters of family Kirstie always approached with
caution, because it usually meant that sooner or later it
led to the subject of her mother's remarriage, and that
too in its time had been another cause for bitter unhappiness. She seldom spoke of it to anyone and did so
only reluctantly now. 'My mother's still alive,' she said,
'but she remarried and lives in South America.'

'While you chose to come and live in Spain with your
grandfather, eh?'

Again Kirstie hesitated before she answered. She
wouldn't deliberately seek his sympathy but there was
something about his present mood that encouraged
confidence. 'It wasn't really a matter of choice,' she told
him quietly, 'although I've never regretted it for a
moment; I love being with Abuelo.' She pulled a rose
from one of the bushes as she passed, and held it to her
nose for a moment. 'My mother's new husband wasn't
very keen on having a fourteen-year-old stepdaughter
around so, as I wasn't really old enough to be left entirely to my own devices, Abuelo asked if I'd like to
come and live with him, and of course I did.'

'Ah!' He sounded as if he understood exactly how she
felt, and once again Kirstie wondered at his capacity for
understanding. 'You like Spain?'

'I love Spain,' she told him with absolute certainty. 'I'm half Spanish, of course, and when I was a child we spent six months of every year here at Casa de Rodríguez, and the rest in Scotland where my father had a business. It's nearly seven years since I came to live here for good, and I feel as if I've always been here.'

'Which accounts for your fierce resentment of me and my family taking over the estate,' he guessed, and went on before she could confirm it. 'I think perhaps you might be less resentful of my youngest brother, however. He's coming home to join the firm next week and he'll be much more to your taste. He's thirteen years younger than I am and very good-looking; what is termed a romantic, which usually appeals to women, I believe.'

The hint of cynicism was more the kind of thing she was accustomed to from him, but in this instance she found herself regretting it rather than resenting it. It was perhaps because she had quite enjoyed those few unexpected moments of confidence that she spoke up as she did, unmistakably on the defensive.

'I can see nothing wrong with being a romantic,' she said, and as they reached the end of the path and stood looking down the ride through the orange grove, he turned and looked down at her thoughtfully.

The shadows of the trees drew deeper, harsher lines on his face, and cast his eyes in enigmatic blackness between their heavy sable lashes. 'It's simply a matter of character, I suppose,' he mused. 'I hadn't much time for romanticism when I was Luis's age; I learned my lessons in a harder school altogether, and also of course I've been around a lot longer. Luis assumes without question that any lovely young woman he meets is not only in need of his protection, but is just waiting to be swept off her feet.'

'He sounds very charming and—and gallant,' Kirstie declared, firmly in favour of the qualities he seemed to be mocking. 'I look forward to meeting him.'

Miguel's eyes glowed darkly as they looked down at her, and something in their depths was making her

strangely uneasy suddenly. 'Oh, I'm sure Luis will find
you enchanting,' he said in a voice that was noticeably
softer and deeper, and she caught her breath when he
reached for her left hand and raised it to his lips. It was
a light, warm caress that stirred unexpected responses
in her and she gazed at him a little dazedly. '*Adios*, Señorita Rodríguez,' he said.

With barely time to recover, Kirstie spoke quickly and
without thinking. '*Adios, señor*, I'll see you tomorrow
morning.'

Miguel stopped and turned, and his eyes were gleaming and faintly mocking. 'Not necessarily,' he said.
'Wasn't it one of the conditions of your coming to work
for us, that you wouldn't have to see me?'

Without giving her time to reply, he turned again
quickly and went striding back along the path towards
the house, leaving her wondering why her own objections to working with him should suddenly seem so dismayingly childish and unreasonable.

CHAPTER TWO

HER grandfather declared himself pleased that her interview had been successful, but Kirstie knew him well enough to guess that deep in his heart he did not relish the thought of his granddaughter going out to work to help support him. She had been telling him about Enrique Montañes and had left him in no doubt that there was one member of the Montañes family at least she was prepared to like.

'He's very nice,' she assured him, 'and nothing like his nephew, except maybe for a certain physical likeness, allowing for about twenty years' difference in age.'

'I understand that the uncle is unable to walk, is that right?' Don José asked, and Kirstie looked at him curiously.

'That's right. His legs were shattered in a car crash three years ago; but how did you know that, Abuelo?'

Her grandfather regarded her steadily for a moment, for he knew all about her feelings towards Miguel Montañes. 'His nephew told me that his uncle was confined to a wheelchair,' he said, 'but naturally I couldn't ask the reason, and he didn't volunteer any.' He looked at her again, and it was obvious that her greater knowledge puzzled him. 'I hope you weren't indiscreet enough to ask,' he said, and Kirstie looked at him reproachfully.

'He mentioned it quite naturally in the course of conversation,' she said as she set the table for their evening meal. Seeing even a glimpse of another side to Miguel had been curiously unsettling, but she was not about to have a complete change of heart on the strength of it. His growing friendship with her grandfather still didn't please her, although she wasn't exactly sure why, and her grandfather was very grateful for his occasional visits. 'You've become very friendly with him, haven't you, Abuelo?' she ventured, and Don José acknowledged it with a slight nod.

His face did not change expression, but a glimpse of imperiousness in his eyes reminded her that he was not accustomed to having his actions questioned, even by her. 'Don Miguel is a good man, whether or not you happen to like him, my child, and I find him extremely interesting company. I see very few visitors and because he's good enough to call on me when he's in this direction, I appreciate his courtesy in doing so.'

'Yes, of course.'

Setting a dish of paella on the table, Kirstie was excused the need to meet his eyes while she served them their meal, but she knew just how closely her grandfather was watching her as she ladled out the steaming food on to their plates. She hoped he wasn't going to question her too closely about her last encounter with Miguel Montañes, for Don José was still very much a supporter of the old virtues of respect and courtesy, no matter how low he might sink financially. He disapproved strongly of her attitude towards Miguel.

Picking up his fork, he sampled the blend of rice, chicken and prawns and his nod of approval pleased her, but not the look in his eyes. 'I hope you've been more polite to him recently, Kirstie. On the few occasions when you've been home and he's called, you've behaved disgracefully. It grieves me that you should be so lacking in good manners towards Don Miguel when he's shown us only courtesy and kindness. Remember he's responsible for you having the position as his uncle's secretary, and I hope you thanked him as you should, by the way.' Kirstie couldn't honestly remember whether she had or not, but she nodded and her grandfather took her word for it. 'Good, I wouldn't like him to think you ungrateful.'

'I'm thankful I'm not working for him,' said Kirstie with a flash of defiance. 'If I'd been required to divide my time between him and his uncle I wouldn't have taken the job, Abuelo; I simply can't—take to him.'

'That's something you've taken no pains to hide,' her

grandfather rebuked her sharply. 'I simply can't imagine why you dislike him so much, Kirstie. He's a very presentable man of good family, and he's no more responsible for the loss of Casa de Rodríguez than anyone else in his family. Less so than I am myself. *Why* don't you like him, child?'

'I don't know.' It was too hard to explain because she didn't understand it herself, and she speared a prawn with her fork before conveying it to her mouth, her eyes dark and resentful. 'He's always so—so arrogant, for one thing, and he treats me as if I'm still in school! Today, if you please, he actually addressed me as "child". Also he's always so—so tolerant he infuriates me!'

'Kirstie!' Don José sighed, shaking his head over her outburst. 'You should be grateful for his tolerance, and as for calling you a child—He's thirty-four years old, and the way you behave must make him think of you as a wilful and badly-behaved child whom he wishes he could take steps to curb in the appropriate manner!'

'Abuelo!' she pouted reproachfully, but she knew her grandfather well enough not to expect him to retract one word of his scolding. 'I suppose you think I should go out of my way to be meekly polite to him because of the—concessions he allows us? Like giving us the freedom of the estate and letting me take out Scheherazade.'

'It would be more appropriate than rudeness,' Don José told her.

But not even to please her grandfather could she commit herself to a change of heart towards Miguel Montañes, and instead she passed hopefully on to another subject, though not one entirely unconnected with the man they had been discussing. 'According to him I shall get along much better with his youngest brother,' she said, and her grandfather looked up for a moment.

'The youngest brother?'

Having steered him away from the older man, she nodded hopefully. 'It seems he's due home from univer-

sity next week and he's to join the family firm. I think
he must have been something of an afterthought, because according to his big brother, there's thirteen years
between them.'

There was a thoughtful look on the old man's face as
he gathered up another mouthful of paella, and Kirstie
wondered what he was thinking. 'So much younger?' he
said. 'Then I hope you will feel better disposed towards
him, child; at twenty-one he's closer to your own age,
and equally eligible, one would think.'

'Eligible?' Kirstie looked up sharply and her pulse was
suddenly more rapid, she realised, as she stared across
the table at him. 'Abuelo, what are you talking about?'

'I know that the middle brother has been married for
some time and has a family,' her grandfather stated
knowledgeably, and as he took a sip from his glass of
wine Kirstie told herself he couldn't possibly be going
to say what she feared he was. 'Neither of the other two
brothers is married,' the old man went on, 'and it's a
situation that has distinct possibilities, my child. I'm
almost seventy-one and if I should go tomorrow I'd be
happier knowing that there was someone to care for
you. A husband with both wealth and breeding is the
ideal answer, and here you have a choice of two.'

'Abuelo, I'm not a thoroughbred horse!' She put
down her fork and continued to stare at him in dismay
and disbelief, not least because she couldn't be absolutely sure he wouldn't mention his wild scheme to one
of the men concerned. 'You can't seriously mean to try
and marry me off to one of the Montañes brothers—I
won't believe it!'

'I can't imagine why not,' her grandfather told her
sternly. 'I am concerned about your future in our present
circumstances, child, and if I can see you married to a
man worthy of joining with the Rodríguez name I shall
die happy. Since the younger brother is so much nearer
to your own age then he would seem the more suitable.'

Kirstie's short burst of laughter bordered on the hys-
terical, and she was shaking her head slowly as she con-

tinued to stare at him. 'Well, thank heaven at least I'm to be spared Miguel!' she said, and Don José frowned.

'I'm only thinking of your good,' he insisted relentlessly, and a little chill ran along Kirstie's spine when she saw the look in his eyes, and remembered how often such arrangements had been made in his early days. 'You must put yourself out to be pleasant to this young man when he arrives,' he went on, 'and don't antagonise him as you have his brother. You're an extremely pretty girl, but a great deal depends on what sort of an impression you make as a person.'

Still not quite able to believe he was serious about it, Kirstie decided to treat it all lightly, and she got on with her meal again, talking lightly and matter-of-factly. 'What *I* think of *him* depends on how much like Miguel he is,' she said. 'According to Miguel he's a romantic, which sounds an improvement, but I don't see myself setting out to seduce him if he isn't my type, Abuelo.'

Her grandfather's stern gaze disapproved of her flippancy, and he was shaking his head. 'Be pleasant and courteous,' he advised. 'That's all.'

'I'll try,' Kirstie promised as she popped in another mouthful of paella, but she didn't dare think he was serious about marriage—especially with Miguel.

The following morning Kirstie was appalled to realise how nervous she was as she walked along the ride to Casa de Rodríguez, and it wasn't entirely due to the fact that she was about to start her first job. Those rather unnerving suggestions her grandfather had made about marriage into the Montañes family had assumed much more serious implications when she lay in bed waiting for sleep to come, and she hoped and prayed he wasn't going to confide his hopes to Miguel during one of their friendly conversations.

She had no intention of getting herself involved with any of the Montañes other than in the way of business, and she would leave her grandfather in no doubt of it. At the moment there were other matters to concern her;

such as whether or not her typing and shorthand speeds
had deteriorated during the two years since she left
school, and if she would be able to cope with unfamiliar
business procedures.

Nor was she quite sure how she should present herself
when she arrived. Did she simply walk in, or should she
ring the door bell and wait to be admitted? She had no
previous experience to guide her, and her legs were
shaking quite alarmingly as she crossed the verandah to
the door. As it happened the decision was taken for her
when the door was opened, as it had been yesterday;
and just as then Miguel Montañes stood in the doorway
watching her with that curiously intent gaze of his.

Her dress was plain blue linen with a fairly high
neckline and half-sleeves, and made her look slightly
older than her years, but was suitably businesslike, she
hoped, and she had brushed her shoulder-length hair
into a glossy black chignon, making her look far more
typically Spanish than he had ever seen her look before.
Low-heeled black shoes rather emphasised her dim-
inutive height, and she hoped he wouldn't realise how
nervous and insecure she felt.

Her grandfather's suggestion nagged uneasily at her
mind again too when Miguel took stock of her businesslike image. His gaze moving over her with explicit
slowness, he took in every item of her changed appearance, and just briefly she believed he smiled to himself.
'Good morning,' he said, stepping back to allow her
inside. 'You're very punctual, Señorita Rodríguez.'

As he had done the previous day, he led the way
across the hall and saw her into the office, then followed
her in and closed the door behind him. She felt immediately more confident at the sight of his uncle and
smiled at him as he put down the telephone receiver.
'Good morning, Señorita Rodríguez, please come in—
you're very punctual.'

His welcome confirmed Kirstie's liking for him, but
she glanced at Miguel, who hovered just behind her,
before she replied. 'I was taught that punctuality is part

of being a good secretary,' she said, 'and I want to make a good start, Señor Montañes.'

'Good, good,' he murmured approvingly while his eyes took note of unmistakable signs of nervousness, and he smiled again, reassuringly. 'Naturally you're a little nervous, *señorita*, but please try not to be, you have nothing to be afraid of here, I assure you. You'll find me less of an ogre than you might expect, I promise you.'

'Oh, but of course you're not!' It was automatic as she made the denial to glance over her shoulder again at Miguel, lingering somewhere in the background, for she wondered why he was still there after his remarks yesterday. Turning back to his uncle, she sought to explain exactly how she felt. 'It's just that this is my first job and I'm so afraid of not knowing what to do, *señor*. I'm a complete beginner.'

'Then just go along at your own pace until you get used to it,' Señor Montañes advised. 'You'll soon pick up a routine, my dear *señorita*, and I'm sure we shall have no difficulty getting along together.' Then he too looked across at Miguel and regarded him quizzically for a moment. 'Don't you agree, Miguel?'

It seemed his nephew suddenly realised he was being involved, and he straightened up, shaking his head and half-smiling. 'It seems it might work,' he conceded. 'You appear to be capable of adapting to circumstances after all, Señorita Rodríguez.'

'Well, of course I am!' she answered pertly, and was aware of Enrique Montañes looking vaguely surprised at the exchange. 'If I'm less than perfect to begin with I hope Señor Montañes will have patience with me.'

'I think the first thing we must get straight,' Enrique Montañes said with a smile, 'is the matter of what you call everybody. We usually solve the problem of all of us having the same name by giving me the senior position as Señor Montañes, and my nephews their various first names. Don Miguel, whom you've met, Don Jaime who deals with our foreign sales and whom you won't see very often, and lastly Don Luis, who will be arriving today.' He took note of Miguel's swiftly arched brows and smiled. 'I haven't had the opportunity to tell you yet, Miguel, but that was Luis on the phone just now. He's arriving today instead of Monday.'

'*I* see!' Something in Miguel's voice caught her attention, but when Kirstie looked around he was watching her and smiling in a curiously dry fashion. 'Oh well,' he said, 'I'll leave you to get on. I may or may not see you again some time, Señorita Rodríguez—*adios!*'

'*Adios*, Señor Montañes.' She caught the look in his eyes when he half-turned in the doorway and hastily corrected herself. 'Don Miguel.'

For a second the dark glowing eyes between their thick heavy lashes held hers steadily, then he turned and closed the door quietly behind him, and quite unknowingly Kirstie let out her breath in a long sigh of relief. 'Now,' said Enrique Montañes, 'shall we begin, Señorita Rodríguez?'

Her first day at work had gone much better than she had dared hope, and Kirstie was quite pleased with herself. Of course Enrique Montañes' patience and understanding had made all the difference, and she was certain she would have found it much less easy with Miguel in charge. Also she had finished far earlier than she expected, and when Enrique suggested she might like to take the mare out for an hour, she had jumped at the chance.

She wasn't accustomed to being cooped up indoors all day, and a ride before supper would revive her, and also give her the opportunity to ponder on how well things had gone so far. There was plenty of time before supper, and she had left a pigeon casserole simmering in the oven all the afternoon, so there was nothing to concern herself with where their evening meal was concerned.

The dainty little Arab mare had been a gift from her grandfather on her eighteenth birthday and Kirstie doted on her, so much so that she had to admit that having to part with her completely would have been almost as much of a wrench as leaving the Casa de Rodríguez. Together with her grandfather they had attended many a *feria*; Don José riding beside her on the sleek, mettlesome stallion that Miguel Montañes now rode. He never rode now and Kirstie missed him more than she dared admit.

In the softer warmth of evening the intricate network of irrigation channels caught the light of the lowering sun and glowed like rivers of wine between the fertile groves. The vastness and fertility of the *huerta* was something that never ceased to enchant her; providing sugar, rice and olives as well as the main crop of oranges, and although the blossom had mostly fallen, the unmistakable scent of oranges still lingered in the air.

A slight pressure of her heels sent the mare forward and, just for a moment, Kirstie thought she felt a slight movement, as if the saddle had slipped a little, but the impression was only brief, and she soon forgot it in the pleasure of her ride. In fact she was enjoying herself so much that the last person she wanted to see was Miguel Montañes looming up on her right.

With any luck he'd be anxious to get home after a hard day in the saddle and would do no more than acknowledge her and then ride on, but at the moment their paths were bound to cross and a meeting was inevitable. Instead of just a murmured greeting and a casual wave, however, Miguel reined in his mount, giving Kirstie little option but to do the same.

'You've finished already?' he asked, by way of a greeting, and she felt herself flush at the tone he used.

'Señor Montañes decided when we finished, I didn't,' she told him. 'He also suggested I might like to go for a ride before supper, and I wasn't going to say no.'

She dismounted and leaned with apparent nonchalance against one of the trees. Watching him from the corner of her eye, she decided that both he and his horse were showing something less than their customary spirit,

and she wondered what had happened to cause it. The
stallion had been ridden hard, that was clear, but Miguel
had a broodingly angry look about him that puzzled
her.

'No, of course not.'

His reply was unexpectedly mild in the circumstances,
and again Kirstie looked at him curiously, taking advantage of his preoccupation with his horse as it drank
from one of the irrigation channels, to study him for a
moment. He was an earthy, virile man and quite alarmingly disturbing at times, so that she stirred uneasily
against the tree trunk, touched by some unexpected sensation she had no control over.

The cream shirt he was wearing was opened almost
half way down and showed glimpses of thick dark hair
and bronzed flesh, and there was a musky, masculine
scent about him that spoke of hours in the hot sun, and
was curiously affecting in the present circumstances. She
was never very long in his presence without feeling the
urge to challenge him, and she looked at him obliquely.
'You don't mind, do you?' she asked.

'That's a foolish question!'

There was a suggestion of suppressed emotion about
him still, and she eyed him thoughtfully. 'Is something
wrong, Don Miguel?'

'Wrong?' He frowned at her for a moment, then
swung down from the saddle and tethered the tired
animal to one of the trees, and she felt her heart give a
quite alarming lurch when he came and leaned with one
hand on the tree behind her. He was hot and dusty and
yet there was a curious excitement about having him so
close so that Kirstie despaired of her own susceptibility.
'You're very observant, *señorita*, I wasn't aware that
my expression gave so much away.'

'Then there *is* something wrong?'

Miguel ran his free hand through his hair. 'I don't
think it's anything that would interest you,' he said, and
she shifted slightly so as not to be quite so close.

'If it concerns the estate I'm interested,' she told him,

and he gave her a brief narrow-eyed look before nodding his head.

'Very well. I've just found it necessary to get rid of one of the workers and it isn't a task I particularly enjoy, however much it was deserved.'

Such sensitivity, she felt, was unexpected in him, and because it surprised her she answered rather absently, 'Oh dear!'

How she could have conveyed disapproval with such an innocuous reply she could not imagine, but Miguel turned his head sharply. 'You don't approve?' he challenged, and Kirstie shrugged.

'I didn't say I didn't approve,' she denied. 'I admit I don't like to think of any of our—the estate people being dismissed, but I can't question your reason or your right. And you don't have to·tell me your reason,' she added hastily.

'For stealing.' Judging by his expression the incident had obviously left a very bad taste, and again she wondered at his sensitivity. 'Apparently it's been going on for some years, but it's never been discovered until now. I've been making regular checks and it came to light during one of them.'

'So it goes back to—our time?'

She didn't like to think of that, but her grandfather had never really been personally involved in running the estate to any great extent. It had always been left in the hands of an overseer, and she wondered if the present régime were more strictly personal in their involvement; it seemed so. What concerned her most about the sacking was if one of their long-term employees was involved, and when she shook her head it was purely and simply because she hated the idea of that. Yet once again, it seemed, she had given him the wrong impression.

'Don't you believe that thieves should be punished, Señorita Rodríguez?' Miguel asked with the resentment that was more usually her prerogative, and she hastened to correct him.

'Well, of course I do! If we'd known about it we'd have done as you have, I dare say; my grandfather is a very—moral man and he would never have let anyone get away with stealing from him.'

'Yet you're still looking at me as if I'm some kind of inhuman monster,' he accused. 'Why?'

'It isn't because you dismissed the man if that's what you think——'

'It wasn't a man, it was a woman!'

Something curled inside her, and Kirstie stared at him in dismay, for she could imagine the feelings of any woman faced with the wrathful vengeance of Miguel Montañes. 'Oh dear,' she said, and again he frowned at her.

'That makes it worse? Being a woman?'

'I just can't help feeling sorry for her,' Kirstie insisted, 'because I think you'd be completely ruthless.'

For a moment he said nothing, but he held her wavering gaze so determinedly that she found it impossible to look away. 'Ah yes, of course, whatever happens, whoever is guilty, I must inevitably emerge as the villain, mustn't I, Señorita Rodríguez?'

'I didn't say that!' she denied, then went on with scant regard for what she was getting into, 'But I can't imagine anyone more guaranteed to put the fear of God into someone than you, and thief or not, I feel sorry for the wretched woman!'

'So!'

A hard, glittering look combined with the weight of the day's tiredness added to his look of unrelenting fierceness, and Kirstie had little doubt that should he lose his temper it would prove no less formidable than the rest of him. Yet it wasn't fear of his anger that made her legs feel so alarmingly unsteady as she leaned more heavily against the tree behind her, and the fingers of one hand curled tightly against the rough grey bark.

There was a curious sense of excitement stirring in her and her pulse was racing in a way that she found alarming. As a man he was almost an unknown quantity, yet in some strange way she felt she knew him better than any other man she had ever met, and her own feelings both puzzled and alarmed her. It was because she felt so uncomfortably out of her depth that her immediate instinct was to get away from him, and the brief glance she gave at her watch was merely to give herself an opening.

'It's time I was getting back,' she said, using her grandfather as an excuse. 'Abuelo will be ready for his supper and I did promise not to be too long.'

It sounded as if Miguel accepted the claim at face value, but a certain look in his eyes suggested he understood just why she was in such a hurry to return home suddenly. 'Yes of course, *señorita*.'

Kirstie turned to untether her horse, but he was closer even than she had realised and there was very little room to manoeuvre. 'Don't bother to wait for me if you're in a hurry to get home, Don Miguel,' she told him, bringing the mare round with difficulty in the small space available. 'I'd rather—I mean I can ride back alone.'

It wasn't until she looked up at him again as she prepared to remount that she noticed his expression. There was a bright hard gleam in his eyes that made her suddenly wary, and when he reached and took the mare's bridle from her she caught her breath audibly. Holding the animal with one hand, he tapped a long Spanish quirt against the toe of his boot, and it was the latter that gave Kirstie most cause for concern as she eyed it warily.

'I'm very tempted to treat you like the spoiled and arrogant child you are,' he informed her harshly, and the quirt tapped more forcefully as he spoke, so that Kirstie watched it with growing apprehension. Noticing it he looked at her with narrowed eyes. 'But don't worry, my self-control is stronger than you fear; if it wasn't you'd find it very difficult to sit a horse for some time!' He stood beside the patient mare, obviously waiting to help her mount, and Kirstie was too dazed to do anything other than obey. 'Come, it's getting late,' he said, 'and elderly gentlemen like to have their supper on time!'

In the circumstances it wasn't really surprising that she felt, but didn't fully register, the fact that the saddle slipped a little when she settled into it. She had intended to check it before she started for home, but not for anything would she mention it now; instead she sat straight as an arrow and murmured only the briefest of thanks before urging the mare forward.

If she had hoped to have a head start and ride off alone, however, she was out of luck, for Miguel was already up and riding alongside her before she had gone more than a few feet. She automatically turned in the direction that would take her back to the stable, but when Miguel joined her he pulled on the mare's rein and turned her aside.

'We'll go back this way,' he decided, 'then you can go straight in and get Don José's supper while I stable the horses.'

'Oh, but there's really no need——'

Her objection was automatic, but it was cut short because he kept a firm hold on the rein and for the mare's sake she yielded. When she again felt the saddle shift slightly sideways as they set off she still said nothing, but rode with her chin in the air and her face turned determinedly forward. Riding at their present rate there was little danger that anything would happen.

They rode in silence, but Kirstie realised that she had never before been quite so aware of her own body, and the reason was the proximity of that virile and masculine presence right beside her. The thin white cotton shirt she wore was one she had worn often, but never before had it so obviously stressed the soft round young curves beneath it; and the fawn drill trousers stretched tautly over smoothly rounded thighs had never seemed so closely fitting on other occasions. Nor did the looks that occasionally came in her direction do anything to ease her selfconsciousness, but only increased it.

'We can make better speed than this!'

She glanced round quickly, startled by Miguel's
sudden impatience, but she wasn't in time to do anything. Obviously he was anxious to get home, for he
slapped the mare briskly across the rump with the quirt
he carried, then did the same to his own horse, and
both animals took off immediately.

'Oh no, wait——'

She felt the saddle begin to slip sideways, but before
she could say any more or slow her animal down, she
was plunged downward and sideways at the same time,
and the ground seemed to rise up and meet her. Fortunately Scheherazade was a sensitive and alert animal and
the moment she felt all was not well she slowed down
and eventually stopped, with her head tossing agitatedly.

Some yards away, Kirstie lay winded, but nothing
worse as far as she could tell, but she lay where she had
fallen with the breath knocked out of her and too stunned to move at the moment. She was vaguely aware, in
the near distance, of the stallion being pulled so abruptly
to a halt that he slid on to his haunches with his mouth
gaping on the harshness of the bit, and she watched
Miguel slide from the saddle and come striding back
towards her, his expression one of mingled alarm and
disbelief.

'What on earth happened?' he demanded, and stood
for a second or two towering over her like a black-
headed Nemesis, and glowering darkly.

Kirstie ached, but she was certain there wasn't anything serious the matter with her, yet when she didn't
immediately answer, Miguel dropped on to one knee
beside her. Her eyes were open, but from that angle
they appeared heavy-lidded and half-closed, and he pressed a hand to her forehead; anxious instead of angry
suddenly.

'Are you hurt?' She shook her head because she was
still too winded to speak, but she made a tentative effort
to sit up and was immediately pushed back again. 'No,
stay where you are until I make sure you're all right.

Does anything hurt? Your ribs or your back?'

'No. No, I'm all right, just winded.'

Her voice was light and breathless and slightly husky, for he wasn't taking her word for it. Large and surprisingly gentle hands spanned her rib cage and checked for damage; working round from back to front and from bottom to top, the backs of his hands touching the warm intimacy of her breasts with the lightness of a caress, so that she held her breath to try and lessen the contact.

Eventually he eased back and looked down at her with dark, fathomless eyes for a moment. 'You seem to be O.K.,' he remarked. 'Can you move your arms and legs?'

Kirstie obligingly moved all four limbs, and it was while her arms were extended that he reached and slipped his hands under her shoulders, drawing her upward until she was within the circle of his arms. Instinctively she put her hands to his chest to keep some distance between them. 'I'm perfectly all right,' she insisted, still in that curiously breathless voice, but Miguel still knelt there.

'Hmm.' His arms held her loosely and his big hands were on her back, the palms warm through her shirt, and she found it much too difficult to meet his eyes. 'How did it happen, Kirstie?' he asked, and her pulse gave a great leap of surprise when he used her first name.

'The girth slipped; I'd felt it move earlier and I meant to have adjusted it before I started back.'

'Then why didn't you?' He was looking at her in a way that made it impossible to meet his eyes for more than a second or two. 'Didn't it slip when you got on just now?'

'A little.'

'And you said nothing!' He was shaking his head, and the long fingers on her back pressed hard for a moment, as if in reprimand. 'Didn't you realise how dangerous it was riding with a loose girth?'

Kirstie admitted it with a slight nod, but said nothing.

She was shaking like a leaf, but it had little to do with the recent fall, she suspected; it was more the effect of that stunningly virile body that now and then touched hers, despite the barrier of her hands, and the steady darkness of his eyes watching her. His hands moved on her back, slowly and lightly, so that the strong brown fingers seemed to stroke her skin through the thin cotton shirt and she instinctively arched her body towards them.

'You're a little fool.' He spoke softly, his voice in direct contrast to the accusation, and Kirstie glanced up through the thick blackness of her lashes. 'You took a quite unnecessary risk of being seriously injured rather than tell me there was something wrong,' he went on before she could protest. 'Isn't that taking your dislike of me to extremes?'

Still she said nothing, but sat with his arms supporting her; aching a little, but nothing that a hot bath wouldn't soon put right, and increasingly aware of how her own body was responding to that dangerous aura of masculinity about him. Then his arms were gone suddenly and he straightened up, reaching down with his hands to help her stand and supporting her with his hands on her arms until he was sure she could stand on her own feet.

'Will you be all right while I check that girth?' he asked, and Kirstie nodded.

She walked slowly over and watched while he carefully examined the buckle and strap, noticing the way he frowned over it, and when he nodded she ventured an opinion. 'Is the buckle worn?'

Miguel looked up swiftly, still frowning. 'Dangerously so; didn't you notice it when you saddled up?'

'I thought it wasn't as good as it might be,' she confessed, and he clicked his tongue impatiently.

'Then you should have had more sense than to use it!'

'And miss my ride?' she parried. 'There isn't another one.'

'Then it will have to either be mended or replaced!'

Kirstie watched him tighten the girth and double the end of the strap back on itself to make it more secure, while she realised with regret that the old sense of resentment was once more raising its ugly head. 'I'll have to wait until I get my first month's salary before I can afford that,' she told him. 'Which means I'll just have to do without my rides, I suppose.'

She hadn't realised how sorry she sounded for herself, but when Miguel had given the strap a last final pull and then turned to face her, there was a gleaming look in his eyes that was all too familiar to her. 'Don't try and play for my sympathy,' he told her. 'You know me better than to expect me to pity you in your poverty!'

The harshness of it stunned her for a moment, and her face flooded with hot colour. 'How—how dare you!' she whispered hoarsely. 'How dare you speak to me like that? I'm not looking or asking for your sympathy, Don Miguel, I never have!'

'Good!'

He took her fury in his stride and surprised her by walking off with the mare and remounting his own horse still holding her rein, while Kirstie stared after him, blank-eyed with amazement. He surely didn't intend to put her afoot so far from home. But he came back to where he had left her, the stallion friskily anxious to get home and jerking at the bit while Miguel reached down a hand.

'Come,' he told her, and Kirstie stared at him. 'You'll have to ride pillion, that girth isn't safe until it's been fixed, and you've surely ridden double before.'

For several seconds she hesitated, her distrust of him refusing to accept the intimacy of riding behind him, while her emotions stirred to almost fever pitch at the thought of being in close proximity to that exciting virile body. His patience growing thin, Miguel thrust the proffered hand under her nose and frowned, and she suddenly saw little point in refusing. The mare was his and he was, she believed, perfectly capable of making her walk home.

Grasping her hand, he swung her up behind him and it was automatic to put her arms around him as he jabbed the stallion into action, the sudden forward motion throwing her against him. They rode in silence, but Kirstie's brain whirled with a thousand different reactions and emotions, and she wasn't sure whether it was relief or regret that she felt when the little white *barraca* eventually came into view.

Miguel dismounted almost before the animal had stopped, and he reached up his hands for her, clasping them strongly around her waist and taking her weight easily. But when she stood on her own feet he still kept a hold on her and she looked up swiftly, then as quickly looked away from that disturbingly steady gaze of his.

'I'll see that a new buckle is fitted as soon as possible,' he told her, and she flushed anew when she recalled her self-pitying remarks regarding having it mended herself when she could afford it. 'In the meantime you'll have to do without your rides, I'm afraid.'

'But if I fixed the buckle the way you did just now——'

'No!' He cut her short and his hands pressed hard into her back. 'You won't take chances like that again; it isn't worth risking injury just to be stubborn.'

'I could ride bareback; I have done.'

Heaven knew what made her go on, but there was something about him that made a challenge irresistible, and he looked down at her for a moment in silence, the glittering darkness of his eyes shivering through her like ice and fire. 'Don't challenge me, Kirstie,' he said softly. 'Whatever your opinion may be, I don't enjoy dealing harshly with women, and especially such a very young woman, but if you goad me too far you may find me more ruthless than even you think.'

Kirstie said nothing, for there was an air about him that suggested he meant exactly what he said. It was completely unexpected when he took her hand in his and raised it to his lips as he had on another occasion lately, and the touch of his mouth was warm and light, lingering slightly, so that her fingers curled automatically in response.

For a moment the deep dark eyes looked directly into hers. 'A girl like you should be married,' he said.

Kirstie's eyes widened and blinked rapidly, for she could hardly believe it of her grandfather that he had confided that preposterous idea to Miguel, and yet it was too much to believe in coincidence. 'If my grandfather said anything to you about that——' Her voice trailed off, because it occurred to her suddenly that she couldn't possibly go on working for the Montañes if they knew about her grandfather's hopes of marrying her to one of them.

'So we're of the same mind, are we?' Miguel said, and scanned her flushed face for a moment with speculative eyes. 'Who does he have in mind, Kirstie—my youngest brother? You'd make a handsome pair, I agree.'

'I don't even know your brother and neither does he,' Kirstie insisted breathlessly. 'And I don't intend getting married to anyone at the moment!'

'You should consider it,' Miguel urged, and he placed his hands on her arms, drawing her towards him slowly so that she instinctively looked up at him.

Her mouth was soft and vulnerable with lips slightly parted, and he touched his own to them very lightly at first. It was when the pressure became more urgent that her breathing got so rapid and uneven, although it was obvious that he held a much deeper passion in check; a passion that he did not give rein to.

'Consider it,' he insisted against her tingling mouth, then suddenly turned away.

Dazedly Kirstie watched him, standing beside the gate into their tiny *patio* as he rode down between the orange trees leading the mare. A tall and stunningly virile figure, and menacing too in some curious way she didn't understand. And she wondered if she was ever going to understand the dangerously affecting character of the man.

CHAPTER THREE

HAVING gone without her rides for a couple of days Kirstie looked forward to going again. The broken girth had been repaired, so Miguel had informed her last night, and she got herself up early the following morning. She had ample time, but just in case she was gone longer than she expected, she left her grandfather's breakfast ready for him.

The mare was as delighted as she was herself that things were back to normal, and Kirstie was so eager to be off that she barely noticed the absence of the stallion from his stall as she led Scheherazade out into the stable yard. Evidently Miguel was an early riser too this morning, and she wasn't too bothered about meeting him as he usually went much farther afield first thing.

The day was already hot as she made for the olive groves, and she reminded herself of the need to keep a watch on the time; something she had never had to concern herself with before. Keeping an eye on the time took a little pleasure out of her ride, but she managed to go quite a distance before it became necessary for her to turn for home, and she was more than half way back when she realised that she was about to have company.

Recognising the familiar sleek lines of Miguel's usual horse, she felt her pulse flutter suddenly in anticipation, but then she realised that although the horse was his, he wasn't riding it. A swift check with her watch warned her that she should go on, but curiosity got the better of her and she deliberately slowed down to get a better look at the rider.

Even at a distance it was possible to detect a definite likeness to Miguel, and it was enough for her to make a guess at who he might be. He looked quite a

bit younger than Miguel, and his hair was more dark
than jet black, but there was a similarity in the features that made her quite certain she was about to
meet Luis Montañes.

She recalled his brother's rather cynical description of
him as a gallant romantic, and it was too much to resist
waiting to see if it was true, which was why she stopped
and waited for him to join her, as he evidently meant to
do. He rode well and came fast, coming right up close
before pulling the big stallion to a halt; a flamboyant
gesture that was obviously done with the object of impressing her, and the look in his eyes was frankly and
unashamedly appreciative of what he saw.

'Good morning, Señorita Rodríguez.' He looked quite
incredibly pleased with himself when her smile confirmed his guess, and he lowered his head almost to his
saddle bow in an exaggerated bow. 'I am right, aren't
I?'

Kirstie smiled, because he was a much different character from his brother. 'You're right,' she agreed.

'Luis Montañes,' he told her. 'But you'll have been
told I was coming I expect.'

'A little earlier than you were expected, I believe, Don
Luis.'

He again bobbed his head in a bow, glowing brown
eyes watching her in a way she could not pretend to
object to. 'If I'd known what was in store for me when I
got here, I'd have come even sooner,' he assured her.
'Are you on your way back, Señorita Rodríguez?' Reminded of the time again, Kirstie nodded. 'Then I'll
come with you, if I may.'

Gallant and romantic had been Miguel's opinion of
his youngest brother, and so far Kirstie could find no
fault with it. He was in fact slightly better looking than
Miguel and more slightly built, with his dark hair worn
long enough to curl up over the collar of a blue shirt
that in no way resembled the practical style his brother
wore.

It was made of some silky material, open at the neck

to display a silk bandana, and the sleeves were full and fastened at the wrist with pearl studs. His short boots were of soft suede with fairly high heels that had silver spurs attached. He was very definitely a romantically attractive figure, and Kirstie suspected he was fully aware of the fact.

He had dark soulful eyes, and as they neared the house he turned them on her as he leaned across and clasped his fingers over hers. 'I'm so sorry you lost your home, Señorita Rodríguez,' he said in a voice that throbbed with emotion. 'It seems so wrong somehow that after having Casa de Rodríguez for so long you now have to live in that tiny *barraca*; I do feel for you, please believe me.'

Rather surprisingly his emotional offer of sympathy caused her more embarrassment than anything else, and Kirstie hastened to deny any need for pity. 'Oh, please don't let it worry you, Don Luis, we manage very well, and we're quite comfortable.'

She recalled uneasily all the times she had let Miguel see her resentment, but Miguel had never been so emotionally apologetic about taking over the house and estate, and nor had he ever looked at her with such big soulful brown eyes as Don Luis did. 'But don't you miss it?' he insisted, and she smiled at him rather vaguely.

'Yes, of course, Don Luis, but there's no use in crying over something one can't do anything about,' she told him, as if she had never cried in the past few painful weeks. 'We're lucky to be still living on the estate, and now that I have a job with Señor Montañes——'

'Brave as well as beautiful,' Luis Montañes said gravely, and Kirstie again merely smiled. She was aware of him watching her with a warmly appreciative gaze that did a lot for her morale, and when they rode into the stable yard at the back of the house, he hurried to help her dismount then took the reins from her. 'I'll see to this for you,' he told her, and Kirstie smiled her thanks, not loath to be waited on for a change.

'You're very kind, *señor*, thank you.'

She hadn't smiled so much for quite a time, she realised, and obviously her smile was something that Luis Montañes found to his liking. For while he stood holding the two animals with both hands, his eyes were fixed on her, warm with pleasure. 'I've already been here two days', he said, 'why haven't I seen you before? I'd willingly have started work with Tío Enrique right away if I'd realised what I was missing!'

Kirstie felt a warm glow of satisfaction as she basked in the blatant invitation she saw in his eyes, and her own eyes smiled teasingly. Flirting was something she could indulge in quite naturally with Luis Montañes, and it seemed too long since she had enjoyed anyone's company as much as she did his. She chose to forget the occasion when Miguel had kissed her because Miguel was not a man one flirted with, he was much too fiery and forceful. Also thinking about Miguel at this particular moment was oddly discomfiting.

'Didn't they tell you there was a new secretary?' she asked, and Luis Montañes pursed a full lower lip before he answered.

'Tío Enrique said you were charming, which is what he says about most women, and Miguel said you were lovely—enchanting, I think was his description of you. But you see, I was judging you on Miguel's usual taste in women and I expected a tall and sophisticated thirty-year-old, not a dainty little creature like you.' For a moment his gaze was speculating rather than soulful and it looked quite at odds with the romantic image. 'When I think about it,' he went on, 'it wasn't like Miguel to remark on your looks, you must have impressed him.'

'I hardly think so,' Kirstie denied swiftly, and regretted the way she coloured so readily. 'Your brother and I have never managed to get along together; we treat each other with a kind of mutual—distrust.'

'Really?' He appeared unconcerned. 'Well, it isn't

important as you don't work for him, is it? On the other hand, you'll be seeing quite a lot of me. I'm to work part of the time with Tío Enrique in the office and the rest with Miguel, and I must say I'm looking forward to the office work more than I am to riding around with Miguel.'

His meaning was unmistakable, and Kirstie felt a flutter of anticipation at the idea of working with him. 'I look forward to it too, Don Luis,' she told him, and wondered why he frowned suddenly.

'Before we go any further,' he stated firmly, 'I insist you forget that Don Luis nonsense. A title may be all very well for my uncle and Miguel, or Jaime, but we're young enough to dispense with ceremony, eh, Kirstie?'

'If Señor Montañes has no objection,' said Kirstie, 'I don't mind in the least.'

'He won't,' Luis assured her confidently.

He had been smiling so self-confidently that Kirstie frowned when she saw the sudden change in his expression, but she had no need to turn and discover the reason when she heard the heavy tread of booted feet coming up behind her. It was typical of Miguel to put in an appearance at a moment like this, she thought, but when she eventually turned and saw how glower-ingly angry he looked, her heart fluttered anxiously. There must be something very wrong for him to look as he did, but her main concern at the moment was whether it was to be herself or his brother who was to take the brunt of his anger.

In a white shirt he looked stunningly dark by contrast, and fawn drill trousers emphasised muscular calves and thighs as he came striding towards them. Even his long legs seemed to express anger, for his gait was taut and stiff and his firm tread had an ominous sound on the hard ground.

He spared no time for pleasantries, but came straight to the point in a harsh, impatient voice. 'Luis, what the devil do you mean by taking my horse? You know I start immediately after breakfast and yet you went prancing off without a thought, working the damned animal up into a sweat before I've even started!'

Kirstie was an unwilling witness, and her sympathy was automatically with the younger brother. Luis had coloured furiously and she knew it was mostly because she had been there to hear Miguel berate him like a thoughtless schoolboy. If she had thought for a moment that she had a chance of slipping away unseen she would have done so, but as it was, from the way Luis was looking at her, uneasily, almost apologetically, she realised she was going to be involved, however unwillingly.

'I thought you'd take the mare,' said Luis. 'I didn't think——'

'That Señorita Rodríguez would be taking the mare,' Miguel finished for him, and Kirstie stirred uneasily.

She felt bound to go to Luis's rescue, whatever risk she took of bringing Miguel's wrath down on her head. Obviously he had known nothing about her taking Scheherazade and so she felt partly to blame for the position he was in. Also he was good-looking and charming and he made her smile as she hadn't smiled for some time; it seemed a good enough reason to risk incurring Miguel's wrath.

'I didn't realise,' she said, coming in quickly before Luis could speak up for himself. 'When I noticed the stallion was gone I automatically assumed you were already out. If I'd known you were going to need Scheherazade, naturally I wouldn't have taken her. But I'll remember in future, Don Miguel, not to take your horses without your specific consent—I'm sorry!'

Her intervention was obviously unexpected, for when Miguel turned to her his eyes were narrowed and gleamingly dark. 'You're as aware as my brother is that the mare isn't any use to me,' he said. 'She's a woman's horse, not a man's; she hasn't the stamina I need for a day's riding.' A deepening of his voice made the rest of his words audible only to her. 'Don't make me responsible for any more sacrifices on your part,

Kirstie, it isn't necessary!'

Kirstie's colour flared hotly and her eyes were bright and angry. She hated him for that jibe about making sacrifices and for the moment did not appreciate that he had made it so that his brother did not overhear. If she had given rein to her temper, heaven knew what the outcome might have been, but in the event it was Luis Montañes who brought a calmer voice to the situation.

'I suppose I should have realised the mare was too light for you,' he said, his eyes on Kirstie. 'I'm sorry, Miguel, but I just didn't think.'

It was impossible for things not to cool down after that, and Miguel's fierce gaze was already less fearsome as he looked at the contrite face of his brother. He sighed and shook his head, then put a hand on Luis's shoulder. 'Try and think next time you feel like running my horse into the ground,' he told him, 'that's all I ask.' Luis stood still holding both horses and looking as if he wondered what to do next. 'If you were going to unsaddle for the *señorita*, you'd better go and do it,' Miguel advised mildly. 'And give Hassan a rub down and then resaddle him for me, will you? I'll have to take him, but I'll give him a while to get his breath back first.'

'Yes, of course.' Luis seemed more than willing to do as he said, and a small flutter of rebellion stirred in Kirstie's breast on his behalf. Then he seemed to recall that he still had some unfinished business, and he half-turned, looking at Kirstie over his shoulder. 'I'll see you again, Kirstie?'

She nodded, aware of Miguel's swiftly arched brows when he noted the familiarity of her name, and her response was quite deliberately encouraging. 'Yes, of course, Luis; *hasta luego!*'

'*Hasta luego!*' The brief look he gave Miguel was slightly but definitely triumphant, then he turned and led the two horses away.

Suddenly aware of the time again, Kirstie yet again found herself unexpectedly under escort by Miguel as they crossed the stable yard, and she wondered if, now that his brother was gone, he meant to remark on their riding together. 'Unless you had breakfast before you came out,' he said, 'you haven't much time; it's already eight-thirty.'

'I know, but I won't take very long. I'll be back here by nine, Don Miguel, don't worry.'

'It isn't my concern if you're late, it's my uncle's,' he told her. 'I just wondered if you'd realised what the time was, that's all.' They approached the arched gateway into the *patio* and he moved closer to allow for them to go through together. 'You think I was too hard on Luis?' he asked, and Kirstie jerked her head round quickly and looked up at him. 'I shouldn't have lost my temper with him, eh?'

Kirstie hesitated, unable to resist saying what she thought, but not quite sure how he was going to react. 'I don't think you should have lost your temper with him while I was there to hear it,' she said in a huskily small voice, and to her surprise she realised he was nodding his head.

'It's true. I don't usually let my temper get the better of me, and I can't think why I did on this occasion.'

It was such an uncharacteristic admission coming from him, that she wasn't sure what to say for a moment. 'I suppose you had a right to be angry when you found both horses gone,' she allowed warily, but again he seemed to accept her opinion and was nodding his head gravely.

'Luis has a lot to learn, but we have high hopes of him,' he observed as they walked through the *patio* gardens. 'The only problem is having him in such close proximity to you while he's learning the business. He has a penchant for pretty girls, and unfortunately he's all too easily distracted.'

'Then I shall do my best not to distract him!'

Heavy-lidded eyes looked down at her, faintly quizzical. 'Is that possible?' he asked, and Kirstie looked up at him, anxious suddenly and prepared to offer assur-

ance that she wasn't very sure she could keep if she
had judged Luis Montañes correctly.

'I take my job seriously, Don Miguel, and I shan't
distract Don Luis during working hours, you have my
word.'

'And out of working hours?' Miguel asked softly.

She met his eyes with her chin angled in a way there
was no mistaking. 'Out of working hours what I do is
my own affair, Don Miguel!'

'Ah!'

'You don't like me being frank!' she accused swiftly,
but it seemed she was mistaken, for he showed no sign
of resentment, even though his eyes gleamed darkly.

'As you say, Señorita Rodríguez,' he said in a voice
so soft it slid like a velvet finger along her spine, 'what
you do in your own time is your own affair. My brother
is very good-looking, and you make a handsome pair;
your grandfather would be delighted, I'm sure.'

Kirstie had forgotten all about that preposterous
idea of her grandfather's until Miguel reminded her,
and her colour was high as she stared at him reproachfully. 'I'm talking about normal friendly re-
lationships,' she insisted. 'Whatever you and my
grandfather think, Don Miguel, I've no intention of
marrying anyone for years yet, and I wish you
wouldn't concern yourself with things that are none
of your business!'

'But you like Luis?'

'Of course I like him! He's pleasant and—and good-
looking and just as gallant as you said he was, but I
don't fall in love as easily as that! We met just a few
minutes ago!'

'But long enough, it seems, for Luis to be smitten,' he
observed dryly, and before she could object further his
fingertips touched her arm and they came to a halt
where the path split two ways. 'You haven't very much
time,' he said, consulting his watch. 'I'll explain to my
uncle that you've been delayed.'

'There's no need!' Kirstie didn't understand why it

disturbed her so much that he seemed to share her
grandfather's readiness to see her married to Luis, but it
did. 'And please—don't say anything about that ridiculous idea of Abuelo's of wanting to see me married—not
to Luis.'

The time was ticking by, but somehow for the moment
it didn't seem nearly so important as it had, and she
caught her breath when a finger lifted her hair from her
neck and let it fall slowly back again, as if its silky softness fascinated him. 'So Don José *does* hope to see you
marry my brother?' he mused, and Kirstie gave a swift
upward glance.

'But didn't he tell you?' He was shaking his head
slowly, and there was a glitter in the dark depth of his
eyes. 'Then how——'

'I suggested you should be married, that was all,'
Miguel told her quietly. 'It was only when you let slip
that Don José was of the same mind that it occurred to
me Luis would seem an ideal choice to him.'

'Oh!' Her thoughts were running wild, trying to guess
who Miguel's own candidate could have been. Not himself, she couldn't believe that, but who? She was still
trying to come up with an answer when she heard him
give a faint sigh as his hand was withdrawn and he
looked at his watch.

'I'd better make your excuses to my uncle after all,'
he said, but Kirstie shook her head insistently.

'No, please don't, there's no need, I can be back here
by nine.'

'And you'll do anything rather than be under even
the slightest obligation to me,' he observed quietly. 'Very
well, Señorita Rodríguez—*adios*!'

Always a man of swift movement, he had turned
and was striding across the *patio* towards the rear
door of the house before Kirstie could draw breath,
and she watched him go with an undeniable sense of
regret. Not only had he been so sure she was refusing
his help because she did not want to be obligated to
him, but he had taken it so much to heart that he had

reverted to the formality of a title instead of calling her Kirstie. And she wondered if he realised that by making such a point of a future affair with his brother, he had done a great deal to make her wary of the very idea.

Don José wasn't accustomed to spending most of the day alone, but he accepted the necessity of it as he accepted all the other changes in his life, and made up to some degree for his solitariness by listening to Kirstie's account of the happenings at Casa de Rodríguez when she came home.

She had been working for Enrique for two weeks and she now had a routine pretty well established, both at home and in the office. Preparing and cooking meals fitted in quite well with working hours, although she had much less free time than she once had. Her grandfather neither offered nor was expected to make any contribution to the running of the house, but on the whole things worked out very well.

While she dished out cod steaks in tomato sauce, Kirstie passed on the latest piece of gossip from Casa de Rodríguez, and Don José showed his usual interest. 'Did you know that Señor Montañes has his daughter-in-law and his granddaughter coming this evening?' she asked, and her grandfather shook his head, obviously interested. 'They're coming for a month, apparently.'

'I've often wondered if he had a family apart from his nephews,' he observed. 'A daughter-in-law, you say?'

Kirstie nodded. 'His only son was killed three years ago in the same crash that killed Luis's parents and crippled Señor Montañes himself, and apparently he was his only child. He has the daughter-in-law to stay with him because he likes to see his granddaughter, but I gather from Luis that the daughter-in-law isn't very popular and she won't let the girl come alone.'

'The fact that the mother comes too suggests that she's a dutiful daughter-in-law,' Don José suggested, but Kirstie smiled as she handed him his plate.

'According to Luis the attraction is Miguel,' she told him, and noticed the way her grandfather frowned over her flippancy. 'Apparently Rosa Montañes has always—liked Miguel, and since her husband was killed she's made quite a play for him.'

'It seems to me,' Don José remarked disapprovingly, 'that Don Luis is being very indiscreet about his family's affairs. Even if it is true that Señora Montañes wants to marry again, and would prefer it to be Don Miguel, he shouldn't talk about it to a stranger. I'm quite sure Señor Montañes wouldn't like it if he knew.'

'Probably he wouldn't.' For a moment Kirstie's eyes gleamed with malicious mischief as she looked across at him. 'I should think Don Miguel would like it even less!'

'Kirstie!'

For once she ignored the rebuke, caught up in the prospect of Señor Montañes' unpopular daughter-in-law pursuing Miguel with marriage in mind. Not for a moment did she consider that he might be a willing victim, it simply seemed to her a kind of poetic justice after some of the remarks he had made recently about her own marriage plans.

'Unless of course she's tall and thirtyish and sophisticated,' she went on. 'According to Luis that's the type Miguel prefers.' He had also told Luis that she herself was lovely—enchanting was his description, according to his brother, but she kept that strictly to herself. A curiously satisfying secret that she wished Luis did not share.

'That young man gossips too much,' Don José insisted, 'and you shouldn't encourage him, my child, it's very wrong.'

'I can't stop him talking,' she objected. 'And incidentally, he's warned me to expect fireworks while she's here; something to do with me being Señor Montañes' secretary, he says, although I can't imagine why it should bother her who her father-in-law's secretary is.'

Her grandfather was slightly more speculative than

critical, she realised when she looked across at him, and
she frowned at him curiously. 'Could it be because there
could be a certain amount of—jealousy?' he suggested.
'You are, after all, frequently in contact with Don
Miguel, my child.'

Despite her efforts, Kirstie knew she coloured furiously. 'That's most unlikely,' she insisted. 'Firstly because if I'm—friendly with anyone it's Luis, not Miguel,
and I don't see Miguel nearly often enough to give even
the most jealous lover grounds for suspicion!'

Her grandfather said nothing, but his expression was
thoughtful, and she thanked heaven that he knew
nothing about those occasions, few as they had been,
when there would have been grounds enough for a jealous lover to object. The uneasy thought still lodged in
her mind the following morning as she cleared away the
breakfast things, although she did her best to dismiss it.
Suggestions like that were so much more disconcerting
when they involved Miguel rather than Luis.

It was while she washed up their breakfast things that
Don José reminded her he had an appointment in town.
It was a rare enough event for him to go anywhere at all
these days, and to Kirstie it was sad that a man who
had once led a busy social life to have dropped almost
completely out of sight because his pride would not
allow him to accept sympathy from his former friends.

'I'm seeing the oculist this morning,' he reminded her,
'but I'll be back in plenty of time for lunch. My appointment is for nine-thirty, and then I have a little
personal shopping to do—I shall be back here by one,
well before you come in for lunch, my dear.'

'And you'll drive carefully?' Kirstie warned.

'Of course, child! I'm still a competent driver even
though I'm nearing my seventy-first birthday.'

A car of some kind had been considered essential even
in their present circumstances, but the one they now
owned was such a small, ramshackle old thing that
Kirstie feared for its survival every time it was on the
road; which admittedly was very rarely. Yet somehow,

despite its contrast to the elegant limousine they had once owned, her grandfather still managed to endow it with a certain air of luxury.

He drove with his head held high as if oblivious of the vehicle's shortcomings. Neatly dressed and well-groomed, Don José proclaimed his breeding to the world, and endowed the decrepit old car with something of his own elegance. When Kirstie looked at him her eyes were suspiciously hazy for, poor or not, however proud and arrogant the Montañes might be, Don José Rodríguez could match them any day, and she was proud of him.

Kirstie had tried not to let herself become agitated, but the longer it was the more worried she became. They always had lunch about two o'clock and her grandfather had been so sure he would be back well before that; it was now after three and he still hadn't arrived. Don José was a man who seldom deviated from his set course, and it was that which troubled Kirstie most, for he was now two hours beyond the time he had set himself.

She had made herself sit down at the table and eat, but she had eaten very little in fact, and at a time when she should have been back in the office she had still not left the house. It was silly to fret so much, yet she couldn't help it, and when she heard the tread of booted feet her head came up swiftly and she went hurrying across the *patio* to the gate. Her grandfather wore shoes, not boots, but she recognised the new arrival easily enough; if Miguel Montañes was there then perhaps there was a message, the little *barraca* had no telephone.

She met him in the gateway and the first thing she noticed about him was the absence of any sign of concern. Whatever her opinion of him, she couldn't believe that had there been a message from the hospital or the police concerning her grandfather, he would be so completely unmoved and just for a moment she felt a sense of relief.

'I saw you through the gateway,' he said. 'Have you

given up working, or have you decided to give yourself the afternoon off? It's gone three o'clock.'

It occurred to her then that he was making for the house, not coming away from it, and if there was any message for her, he probably wouldn't know about it. In the meantime he obviously expected some kind of explanation for her being so late going back to the office, and Kirstie hastily gathered her wits about her.

'Yes, I know,' she said. 'I'm just coming.'

It was just possible that her grandfather had met someone he knew and was having lunch with him, she supposed, although she thought it unlikely and she toyed with the idea of confiding her fears to Miguel. She might have done too if he hadn't looked at her so impatiently, as if her lingering there still annoyed him. When she got back to the office she'd tell Señor Montañes and see what he had to suggest.

'I'll just get my handbag and lock up,' she said, making a determined effort to pull herself together, and Miguel looked vaguely surprised.

'Isn't Don José home?'

Again she was tempted to confide in him, but instead she merely shook her head as she turned back into the cottage. 'He went to the oculist,' was all she said.

It was apparently enough to satisfy him, for by the time she had fetched her bag and locked up the cottage he was already back in the saddle and moving off. Kirstie followed, but several times as she walked between the rows of orange trees to the house, she glanced back over her shoulder. There was still no sign of the little car, and as she passed through into the gardens her heart was pumping anxiously and she had decided that she definitely must do something about it.

So convinced was she that something had happened to her grandfather that her eyes were hazy with tears and she didn't see Miguel until she was virtually on top of him. He had just come out of the house and he stood for a moment regarding her curiously. 'Kirstie?'

When she looked at him and he saw the tears in her

eyes, compassion overcame impatience and he moved a little closer, his attitude suggesting that he wanted to reach out and pat her hand consolingly. The gesture she made of drawing a hand across her eyes was quite automatic, but it had an irresistible appeal, and she had no idea how thin and uncertain her voice would sound.

'I—I came as fast as I could; it isn't very much after three.'

'Oh, for heaven's sake!' She swallowed hard and caught her bottom lip between her teeth because she was about to make a fool of herself by crying if she wasn't very careful, and that was the last thing she wanted to do. Then two strong and undeniably comforting hands curved about her upper arms and his voice was suddenly much more gentle as he drew her towards him and looked down into her face. 'What on earth is the matter, child? Are you ill?'

She could forgive him calling her child, Kirstie decided, but her carefully nurtured self-control crumbled in the face of his gentleness. 'It—it's Abuelo——'

'Don José?' His hands squeezed her arms lightly in encouragement. 'What's wrong, Kirstie? Has something happened to him?'

In the event it proved much more easy to confide in him than she had thought, and she did so in a huskily unsteady voice that she did her best to control. 'He—he left quite early this morning and he said he'd be back about one, in plenty of time for lunch.' The tears flowed, despite her efforts and she shook her head. 'Something must have happened or he'd never have stayed so long without letting me know.'

'No,' Miguel agreed with a confirming nod. 'No, he wouldn't.'

The look in her eyes appealed for his understanding, although she couldn't doubt now that he did understand. He looked down at her for a moment, then stroked one hand lightly over her silky hair, and she could not in all fairness blame him for the reproach in his voice. 'Oh, Kirstie, why didn't you tell me this when I

spoke to you back there?' he asked softly. But he knew,
Kirstie thought; he knew why she hadn't confided in
him, and she regretted it as much as he seemed to. 'We'll
go and make some telephone calls,' he told her, taking
her arm and turning her into the house. 'Come on, little
one, you have no reason yet to think the worst, so dry
your tears, eh?'

Together they went through into the cool familiarity
of the hall, and while Kirstie stood anxiously by, Miguel
made the promised calls. He rang the oculist first, who
confirmed that Don José had kept his appointment and
left to do some shopping. Kirstie wasn't certain whether
she should be reassured or not by the fact that there
had been no accident reported involving anyone of Don
José's description; nor had the hospital any new admission that filled the bill.

She stood beside Miguel with her hands clasped
tightly together while he dialled another number, and
looked up at him enquiringly. Seeing how tense she was,
he pressed one of his own big hands over hers and
smiled. It was the first time she remembered seeing him
smile as he did then, and it made an unbelievable difference to that stern face, giving her a glimpse of another
man behind the autocratic façade.

'That car of your grandfather's is much more likely
to be the victim than he is himself,' he suggested with
an attempt at lightness, 'so I'm trying the garage. It's
just a chance, but one worth taking.'

'Oh, but of course, I hadn't thought of it being just
the car broken down.'

In fact she had been so certain that something had
happened to her grandfather that she hadn't given a
thought to it being nothing more serious than that ramshackle old car giving out, and while Miguel listened to
someone at the other end of the line, she watched him
hopefully. Then he was describing her grandfather's car
with surprising accuracy, and looking at her only occasionally to confirm some detail.

She waited, holding her breath and trying to still the

urgent thudding of her heart. Confirmation wasn't long in coming, and she perked up visibly when Miguel nodded, obviously satisfied with what he heard, so that by the time he put down the receiver her hand was curled tightly over his arm and she looked up at him anxiously.

'It's all right, Kirstie.' His eyes glowed with satisfaction and filled her with a warm comforting feeling. 'It wasn't an accident, the car simply broke down and had to be towed to the garage. It happened right in the busiest part of town and there was some difficulty getting the towing van there. Why you've heard nothing is because Don José has been trying for the last couple of hours to get through to this number and found it engaged each time. It was probably my cousin making some of her interminable calls to her friends. Eventually he gave up and he's now on his way home by bus.'

Her throat was so constricted that her words were barely audible, and the relief she felt was much more emotional than her rather formal words suggested. 'Thank—thank you, Don Miguel.'

In fact her relief was indescribable, and Kirstie felt a sudden need to hold on to something or someone, because it left her feeling strangely weak and unsteady. She might have instinctively leaned towards him, she couldn't honestly have said for certain, but it was completely unexpected when a hand slipped across her shoulders and she was drawn into Miguel's enfolding arms.

Her face burrowed against the broad comfort of his chest, and she closed her eyes for a moment, while the tears she had done her best to prevent squeezed from beneath the lids and made small damp patches on his shirt. The irony of it being Miguel to whom she turned for support did not yet strike her, and she was conscious only of the infinite pleasure of being in his arms.

'There's no more to cry about.'

His voice was quietly reassuring but slightly muffled, as if his face was smothered by her hair, and the hand that rubbed back and forth across her shoulders aroused those same dangerously exciting sensations again. The strong steady beat of his heart thudded against her cheek, and the hands that lay flat-palmed on his back touched warm flesh through his shirt. She was trembling, but she told herself it was only relief, yet did not for a moment believe it.

'Kirstie?' A big hand cradled the back of her head, the thumb moving back and forth on her nape. 'It's all over, so dry your eyes, hmm?'

'I—I'm sorry.'

Her voice was muffled, but she stirred and lifted her head. She was incredibly reluctant to move, although she wouldn't like Miguel to realise it, and she shook back her hair from her face but didn't raise her eyes. Then he slid a hand under her chin and raised it so that he looked directly down into the hazy blueness of her eyes for a moment.

'Are you O.K.?' he asked, and Kirstie nodded. 'Then you'd better go and give your grandfather his lunch while I explain to my uncle what's been happening. Right?'

Briefly she looked up at him. 'You don't mind?'

'I don't mind,' Miguel assured her quietly, then once more slid his hand under her chin. 'You were going to ask my uncle to help you, weren't you, Kirstie?' She hesitated, then nodded, knowing he wouldn't believe a denial, and he sighed, shaking his head slowly. 'Well, at least you eventually trusted me,' he remarked, and Kirstie looked up.

'I'm sorry,' she whispered.

He made no reply, but after a second or two he bent his head and touched his lips to hers, so lightly at first that she sensed only the warmth of his breath; then suddenly more firmly. An encircling arm pressed her close to the compelling strength of his body until she felt herself yield and flex towards him, and she clung as long as she could to the lingering excitement of his mouth.

He gazed down at her for a moment and a hand

cradled the back of her head still, his eyes glowing darkly
in a way that sent shivers through her whole body.
'You'd better go and see your grandfather,' he told her,
'and I'll pacify my uncle; he probably thinks by now
that you've deserted him.' The arms were withdrawn,
leaving her with a strange sense of loss, and he lightly
brushed a wisp of hair from her cheek with one fingertip.
'*Adios*, Kirstie.'

'*Adios!*'

He was gone with his usual swiftness and she
answered him automatically as she watched him go
striding across to the office to tell Enrique Montañes
why she was going to be so late. It was only when she
turned to go that she realised she in turn was being
watched, and something in the way the woman looked
at her brought swift colour to her cheeks, for she suspected she had been there for long enough to have seen
Miguel kiss her.

The woman stood in the doorway of what Kirstie
remembered as the dining *salón*, and she looked to be
about thirty years old. She was fairly tall with slender
rounded hips and a full bosom, and her hair was gleaming black. She had broodingly dramatic good looks and
near-black eyes that were narrowed and glittering as she
fixed them on Kirstie; so sharp with dislike that Kirstie
knew without doubt that she was looking at Señora
Rosa Montañes. Her employer's daughter-in-law, and
the woman who, according to Luis, had designs on
Miguel.

If Miguel had noticed her there, he had given no sign
of it, and while Kirstie was instinctively glancing across
at the office door she heard another door slam violently.
The woman was gone, but that glittering black look of
dislike was not easy to forget, and Kirstie wondered if
Miguel had any idea of the violent passions he had
aroused when he kissed her.

Heaven forbid that Rosa Montañes should take it into
her head to extract revenge for what had surely been
meant as no more than an added reassurance after the

shock of her grandfather. Luis had promised her fireworks during his cousin's stay, but she hadn't anticipated anything like Miguel's kiss, or the fact that there
would be a witness to it. And just for a moment she
admitted to feeling afraid.

CHAPTER FOUR

LUIS MONTAÑES was not the type to be deprived of his riding simply because his brother had prior claim to the only horse, and within a couple of weeks of his arrival he had bought himself a beautiful dark Arab gelding. It was a typically extravagant gesture, Kirstie suspected, for Luis as the youngest of the Montañes brothers was used to getting what he wanted, and he enjoyed his riding.

Mostly he accompanied Kirstie, but occasionally she went alone and, although she enjoyed Luis's company, she had to confess to enjoying her solitary moments too. Alone she could imagine that things were as they had been before the advent of the Montañes, and she still liked to pretend that Casa de Rodríguez was still hers and her grandfather's.

Her feelings towards the Montañes had begun to change lately, she had to admit, and it was mostly due to Luis's obvious attraction to her, for he made her feel as she hadn't felt for some time. She saw less of Miguel than she did of Luis, although he still called to see her grandfather occasionally, and recently she had got the impression that there might be some kind of business deal going on between them. It was just an impression she got, but if Miguel did put a little profitable speculation her grandfather's way it would be very good for his morale, and she would be grateful to him for it.

It was sometimes hard to believe she had been working for Enrique Montañes for nearly three weeks, and hardly less credible that in the several days Rosa Montañes had been there she had seen nothing more of her after that one brief glimpse in the hall. She had seen Enrique's granddaughter a couple of times, but had never actually met her.

Margarita Montañes was fourteen years old, but although she was still so young she gave promise of being just as darkly sultry as her mother. Either the girl was very shy or she had no desire to recognise her grandfather's secretary, for when Kirstie had ventured a greeting one day, she had received nothing but a long hard stare in return. In all probability the girl's mother was responsible for her attitude, so that Kirstie made allowances for her on that account.

The evening meal had taken less time than usual, so Kirstie had decided to fetch Scheherazade and take a leisurely ride through the groves before dark. The mare picked her way over the familiar ground, her hooves clicking flintily on the stones and her ears pricked for whatever sounds invaded the evening stillness.

It was a soft whinny of warning from the mare that brought to Kirstie's attention the fact that they were not the only ones abroad, and she narrowed her eyes against the lowering sun to try and see who it was. The horse was Luis's handsome gelding, but the rider was unmistakably a woman, and to Kirstie that suggested Rosa Montañes, and she could think of no one she would rather not meet.

There was a haughty angle to her head and, as the distance between them lessened, Kirstie was able to notice details of the rather masculine-looking garb she was wearing. Tailored breeches and long boots were worn with a plain fawn shirt and with a flame-coloured bandana flaunting about her throat to give a touch of flamboyance that proclaimed her very feminine despite her costume. And when she saw her, Kirstie wondered if this was the kind of woman that Luis meant when he had described Miguel's taste.

Her first instinct was to turn aside, but that might have suggested she was nervous of meeting her, and Kirstie had her pride too. In fact they were practically on the perimeter of the Rodríguez estate and she couldn't go much farther without turning back or aside. Uncertain what to do for the best, she stopped and dismounted in the hope that the other woman would simply ride on by.

But it was obvious that Rosa Montañes had no intention of riding on by. Instead she advanced to where Kirstie had tethered the mare and then sat looking at the animal for a moment while Kirstie stood with her back against a tree and tried to appear nonchalant. When the dark eyes were eventually turned in her direction she noticed that they were heavy-lidded and frankly assessing, and the gelding was moved a pace or two closer, while the haughty scrutiny continued.

'Good evening, *señora*.'

She had received no encouragement, but Kirstie was polite from habit, though it seemed the greeting was to be ignored, and the unfriendly eyes continued to watch her. 'So you're the secretary!'

The harsh voice conveyed unmistakably that secretaries were not a breed she was normally called upon to recognise, and Kirstie felt the colour in her cheeks rise with a curl of anger that churned in her stomach. She kept a firm hold on her temper because she wasn't anxious to quarrel with her employer's daughter-in-law, but it wasn't easy.

'I'm Señor Montañes' secretary, *señora*,' she acknowledged quietly, and the tall figure on the horse seemed to draw itself up even more haughtily.

'And I am his daughter-in-law,' she was informed, with the obvious expectation of impressing her.

Kirstie didn't bother to admit that she already knew her identity, but simply introduced herself more fully. 'I'm Kirstie Rodríguez; how do you do, Señora Montañes?'

'That outlandish name—you're half foreign, I believe Luis said.'

The tone of her voice made it an insult, and Kirstie clenched her hands in an effort to contain her temper. 'My mother is Scottish, *señora*, and my father was Spanish.'

'And your grandfather is the old man who lives in the *barraca* at the end of the ride.'

The curling lip and scornful eyes almost goaded Kirstie to rashness, and she looked up with bright angry eyes, all the pride of the Rodríguez in the angle of her head. 'My grandfather is Don José Lorenzo Delgado Rodríguez, *señora*; our family have lived here for well over two hundred years!'

'But not always in a *barraca*, I hear!' Rosa Montañes jeered.

On the brink of losing her temper, Kirstie suddenly realised that she was being deliberately goaded into doing just that, and with the greatest of effort she held tightly to her composure and answered as quietly as she could. 'Not always in a *barraca*, *señora*.'

'I just hope you appreciate how lucky you are to be allowed to stay on the estate,' she was told, and half-turned to indicate the mare that was tethered the other side of her. 'Is that your animal?'

In the first place Kirstie had instinctively nodded agreement, then recalled suddenly that it was no longer true and hastily corrected herself. 'No, not strictly speaking, not now,' she admitted reluctantly. 'She belongs to—the Montañes.' In fact she wasn't exactly sure who to attribute with ownership of the horses, although she suspected they were Miguel's personal property and not literally part of the estate.

'I see.' Narrow eyes watched her closely. 'And does anyone know you—borrow it?'

'Yes, of course they know!' Kirstie's temper flared, because there was no mistaking the implication and she'd stood just about as much as she intended to. 'I have permission to take Scheherazade whenever I want her; she isn't suitable for Mig—Don Miguel and he's told me to go on using her as if she was still mine! He's been very understanding about it.'

It was, she realised, the first time she had given Miguel credit for the concession, but that brief slip of the tongue over his name had been noticed and the glitter in Rosa Montañes' eyes told her how much it was resented. 'Ah yes, Don Miguel,' she drawled softly. 'I have no doubt you find him very—understanding. I suppose he was being understanding that day I noticed you together in the hall!'

She had been half expecting something to be said about that sooner or later, Kirstie realised, but she refused to admit that Rosa Montañes had any right to make an issue of it. That brief kiss had been a very personal thing between herself and Miguel, and she disliked this woman having been a witness to it. Obviously it had made a very deep impression on Rosa Montañes, because she could still look furiously angry about it even four days after it happened.

Still somehow managing to control her own anger, Kirstie realised that she wouldn't be able to for much longer in the face of such deliberate provocation. 'I assume you're referring to the day my grandfather's car broke down,' she said. 'He was gone so long, I felt sure he'd had an accident, and Don Miguel was very helpful in ringing round to garages etc. I was very grateful to him.'

'Oh, I'm quite sure you were!' Rosa Montañes declared harshly. 'You were so grateful you couldn't wait to throw yourself into his arms; a rather demonstrative way of expressing gratitude, I would have thought!'

Kirstie took a long deep breath and clung grimly to the remnants of her self-control. 'You misread the whole situation, Señora Montañes,' she insisted in a voice that shivered with anger, but Rosa Montañes would have none of it, and her eyes blazed at her furiously.

'I think not! I saw you throw yourself into his arms; I'm not a fool, *señorita*, and nor am I blind!'

'But you *are* mistaken!' Kirstie wished she was more certain whether or not she had actually leaned towards Miguel in those first few moments of relief, and therefore prompted him to put his arms around her. But one fact she could be very sure of, and she stressed it unhesitatingly and with no thought for the consequences.

'As for that kiss, Señora Montañes, that was Miguel's idea entirely and nothing to do with me!'

'You bitch!'

It was a second or two before Kirstie realised that by using Miguel's name without the formality of a title she had probably brought matters to a head. Rosa Montañes was so furiously jealous that she was even prepared to overcome the normal pride of her kind and screech like a fishwife in her fury.

'You'd better be careful,' she warned. 'Don't try to be clever with me, you little bitch, or I'll make you sorry for it! You've got Luis running after you at the moment, so let that be enough for you, and stay away from Miguel or I'll make you wish you had! Do you understand me?'

Kirstie was trembling, but it wasn't with anger alone, she realised. Such violent emotions were a new experience in her young life and she was prepared to believe that Rosa Montañes was not making empty threats. Deep down she felt fear and apprehension, although she would never have admitted it, and especially not to this woman.

'You have no right to speak to me like that,' she objected, but her objections were waved scornfully aside.

'I have every right to speak as I wish,' she was told. 'You're my father-in-law's secretary—an employee of the estate, nothing more, and I venture to suggest that he places more value on my opinion than on yours, *señorita*! You'd be better advised to remember your place or I might suggest he gets rid of you!'

'Oh, but he wouldn't, not without good reason!'

Kirstie had been sure when she answered so impulsively, but something in the hard black eyes of Rosa Montañes suggested she knew differently. 'Don't be a fool!' she told her in a flat harsh voice. 'Don't you know how he dotes on his only grandchild? I don't think he'd think your services as secretary were worth losing touch with my daughter—his granddaughter. Remember that the next time you feel like creeping into Miguel's arms!'

'Oh, but you couldn't!' Kirstie was stunned for a moment, for there was an almost fanatical light in Rosa Montañes' eyes. At any moment now, Kirstie thought wildly, she's going to lash out at me, and she again felt the chilling touch of fear. But still it was the enormity of the threat that troubled her most, and she stared up at the other woman in blank disbelief. 'You surely wouldn't blackmail him with taking away his granddaughter,' she protested huskily. 'It would be wicked—inhuman.'

Near-black eyes snapped with fury, and the reins were gripped tightly until her knuckles showed bone-white. 'It's time you were taught a lesson, Señorita Secretary! If the mare belongs to the estate then I don't see why I should have to borrow a horse when this one is available! I'll take it back with me and you can walk; let's hope, you'll learn some manners at the same time, and some humility! You no longer own Casa de Rodríguez, you and that old man, you're peasants living in a *barraca*, and it's time you learnt your place!'

'No, you can't do that!'

It was the work of a moment for Rosa Montañes to reach down and unhitch the mare and there was no time for Kirstie to do anything, even if she could have got past her. The mare was pulled roughly round and heels jabbed sharply into the gelding's flanks, urging him forward, and Kirstie was left fuming and helpless as the little cavalcade moved off. Frustration made her burn with anger, although she faced the fact that Rosa Montañes probably had more right to the use of the mare than she had herself in the circumstances. Her own right was simply a fantasy that Miguel had fostered out of compassion.

It always seemed to come back to Miguel, and for a moment the old feeling of resentment arose again. If he hadn't kissed her, then Rosa Montañes would have had no cause to be so furiously jealous; and yet when she recalled the moment when she stood in the circle of his arms and felt the touch of his mouth on hers, Kirstie found it hard to wish it hadn't happened, whatever upheaval it had caused.

She seemed to have walked for miles, and yet it couldn't be so very far in reality, but Kirstie wished she could have foreseen a walk back before she rode so far. The smart brown leather boots she wore for riding pinched unmercifully when she walked in them, and her mood worsened with every painful step.

She blamed herself for not having made more of an effort to stop Rosa Montañes from taking the mare; she blamed Rosa Montañes for being so insanely jealous, and eventually she blamed Miguel for being the original cause of the whole thing. It was at that point that she noticed him in the distance, riding towards her along the dusty track between the trees, and she watched his approach with mingled anger and relief.

The fact that he had Scheherazade on a leading rein made it inevitable that he had seen Rosa Montañes, she thought, and it made her ponder on what kind of a mood he was likely to be in. How had the other woman explained her possession of the mare? she wondered, and hoped it had not been without a certain amount of embarrassment.

Seeing he was bringing her her horse, Kirstie saw no point in walking any farther and she leaned back against a tree to take as much weight as possible off her feet. Her anger had already diminished to some extent, and she was as much curious as anything as she watched him coming, lowering her eyes when he came to a halt and sat looking at her for a moment before he dismounted.

He tethered the stallion and brought the mare with him across to where she stood. 'Are you all right?' he asked, flinging Scheherazade's rein carelessly around a branch, and Kirstie nodded.

'My feet hurt, that's all; these boots weren't made for walking in.'

He took note of the dark look in her blue eyes and the slight thrust of her lower lip, and shook his head.

'And you're angry,' he said.

'I am!' She left the support of the tree, wincing when she took the weight on her tender left foot. 'What do you expect me to be but angry? I've just been firmly put in my place, so I was informed, and I shouldn't think it's an experience anyone enjoys!'

'Rosa?'

He knew perfectly well it was Rosa, and the look Kirstie gave him condemned him for even asking. 'Of course!' she said, and brushed dust from her trousers with quick jerky movements of her hands. 'You know it was, you must have seen her come back with my horse!'

'I saw her come back with your horse,' Miguel agreed in a voice that suggested he wasn't about to offer sympathy. 'But all she would say was that you needed to be taught a lesson and she'd put you afoot; I didn't stop to question her, I brought the mare back for you instead.'

'Thank you!' Rashly impulsive as always, she didn't pause to think before she went on, 'Although in the circumstances it might have been more tactful to have sent someone else with her, since you were the reason I was being put in my place!'

'*I* was?' Kirstie was already regretting having been so outspoken, but there was nothing she could do to avoid the steady gaze he fixed her with. 'I think you'd better tell me the rest, having gone so far, Kirstie.' When she instinctively shook her head he gripped her arms and gave her a slight shake. 'What are you holding me responsible for now, eh?'

She used her hands in a vaguely helpless gesture, for it was embarrassing to have to tell him the cause of Rosa Montañes' jealousy. But the look on Miguel's face was enough to tell her that he wasn't going to let her off, and she sighed resignedly. 'It really wasn't—I mean there was really no need for her to make so much fuss about it. You remember the day Abuelo's car broke down and you made all those calls for me?' He nodded, and she flicked the tip of her tongue swiftly across her lips. 'Well, it was afterwards—she saw you kiss me.'

'Oh, I see.' He sounded so unconcerned that for a moment Kirstie stared at him; as if it had been of so little importance that he had almost forgotten about it, and her senses rebelled at the very idea.

'Oh, I realise it wasn't anything important to you,' she declared, 'but Señora Montañes took rather a different view! I must admit I can see her point to some extent when she has such a—a personal interest, but considering it was none of my doing I don't see why I should be the one who has to bear the brunt of her temper!'

Miguel was eyeing her narrowly and his fingers gripped her arms more tightly, so that she shrugged protestingly. 'A personal interest?'

He asked the question quietly, but the softness of his voice was in direct contrast to every other aspect of him, and because his mood was affecting her, she was drawn deeper and deeper into indiscretion. 'Of course I've heard that she considers you her own private property, and if Luis hadn't told me, I'd have had proof enough just now!'

'Her behaviour was proof of nothing except a woman's dislike of a younger and prettier woman,' Miguel argued harshly. 'And Luis should have better things to do with his time than discuss me—or anybody else in the family—with you!'

'The hired help!' Kirstie observed bitterly, and was appalled to realise how much it hurt to hear him speak as he did. 'At least you see eye to eye with her about that!'

Anxious to escape, she reached blindly for the mare's rein, but before she could unwind it from the branch, Miguel's hand closed around her wrist and she was swung round to face him again. 'The hired help,' he agreed in a flat, harsh voice, 'if that's how you want to think of yourself, but don't attribute the idea to me! You're always so determined to put yourself in the part of the downtrodden innocent, aren't you, Kirstie?' His eyes glittered darkly at her and she was shivering; affected by the proximity of him and by the emotion charged atmosphere between them. 'The hired help!' he mocked, and she shook her head protestingly.

'It—it's how you see me—you and Señora Montañes,' she insisted huskily.

She was pulled firmly against him suddenly and gasped aloud at the unexpectedness of it. His arms had the unyielding hardness of steel, and there was no defence against the mouth that forced back her head with the fierceness of its pressure on her lips. She made only a small murmur of sound, but the heat of his body burned her like fire, and the stark, overt virility of him was an assault that made her own more vulnerable softness flinch in the first few seconds, before it inevitably yielded as he bound her still closer.

He had kissed her before on a couple of occasions, but nothing had prepared her for anything as fierce and breathtaking as this. Her strength seemed to have drained away and left her too weak to stand alone, and the violent beat of her pulse made sane reasoning impossible. It was like being submerged in a sea of flame and unable to draw breath, and she clung to him helplessly.

He released her mouth only very slowly, lingering on her parted lips while her breath fluttered unevenly, and only slowly did she return to reality. As she tried to clear her head, two big hands clasped her face between their palms and heavy-lidded eyes watched her mouth with a burning intensity for a moment before he spoke.

'Why do I always allow you to get under my skin?' Miguel whispered, and she vaguely noticed an unsteadiness in his voice, a huskiness deep in his throat that was incredibly affecting. She would have questioned his meaning, but he pressed his mouth again over hers and silenced her. 'You do it all the time,' he told her, 'and I ought to be on my guard against it.'

The pulsing warmth of him was still too close to make rational thinking possible, and there were so many sensations coursing through her body that she had never known before; yet she could find nothing about him that had changed. Vaguely she began to wonder how much more jealous Rosa Montañes would be if she had witnessed those last few moments, and yet she found it hard to regret even a moment of it.

A light pressure of fingertips on her cheeks made her glance upward, and she thought she had never before seen quite that look in his eyes, yet when he spoke his voice sounded quite normal again. 'Shall we go back?' he asked, and she automatically nodded agreement.

Somehow the normality of his voice and the matter-of-factness of the question suggested that he viewed what had just occurred with no more seriousness than he had that last occasion, and she twisted her head sharply sideways to free herself of his hands. Keeping her eyes downcast and her head low so that he could not see how flushed she was, she thanked heaven that the light was going rapidly, and that soon it would be dark.

The sun's glow spilled like blood over the pattern of irrigation channels and rice-fields, and among the trees the *grillos* were tuning up for the evening concert, shrilling harshly in the blood-red dusk. They were familiar sights and sounds, and yet for once Kirstie did not feel the sense of quiet she usually did in these circumstances.

Turning to mount, she found Miguel at her elbow and accepted his help without a word, catching her breath at the strength of those big, capable hands. 'Abuelo will think I've got lost! she said in a voice she strove to keep steady. But as they rode in silence back through the groves full of dark shadows, Kirstie wondered if, just for a few moments, she hadn't been utterly and completely lost.

'I'd like to know exactly what happened,' said Luis, 'and

I'm hoping you'll tell me, Kirstie.'

Last evening's episode was the last thing Kirstie wanted to talk about, and she did her best to shrug off his curiosity. Although she had already learned enough about Luis to realise he had the same stubborn persistence as Miguel when his mind was made up, and she hadn't really much hope of putting him off. 'Oh, it was nothing much,' she insisted.

'It must have been something,' Luis argued, 'I saw Rosa's face when she came in. What on earth had you done to make her look as furious as she did, Kirstie?'

Rosa Montañes' anger on that occasion, Kirstie thought, would have been because Miguel had gone looking for her, but she didn't say as much to Luis; only did her best to put him off. 'I didn't do anything,' she insisted. 'It was all rather silly.'

'To do with Miguel?' Luis guessed, then provided his own answer. 'Yes, it must have been to do with Miguel, nothing else would get Rosa into such a state. So—what was it, Kirstie?'

Kirstie sighed, resigned to the inevitable. 'Do you remember about a week ago my grandfather had some trouble with his car and I was worried in case he'd had an accident? Well, maybe you didn't hear about it, it wasn't really important to anybody but me, but at the time I was sick with worry and Miguel was very good about making enquiries for me. When it was all over I felt a bit—shaky with relief, and——'

'And Miguel put a steadying arm around you, I suppose,' Luis guessed, and Kirstie was of no mind to disillusion him, although Rosa Montañes might see fit to some time. 'He would, but thank heaven he wasn't any more effusive, my lovely; I'd hate to think Rosa had any more serious grounds for being jealous. She's got a wicked temper and she really does mean to marry him eventually.'

Kirstie slipped her fingers under the head of a yellow rose and bent her face to its perfume. 'Does Miguel know that?' she asked.

Luis was frowning, she could tell it even without looking at him. 'I imagine so by now,' he said, and hesitated for a moment before he went on. 'Kirstie, you and Miguel have some kind of feud going between you, haven't you? I gathered when I came here first that you weren't exactly on the best of terms, but this thing with Rosa seems to put a rather different complexion on things. *Do* you still dislike him?'

'Not as much as I did.' She made the admission cautiously, because she feared it might give Luis the wrong impression, but it was quite true, she realised. 'It's a bit difficult to—fit him in,' she went on to explain, almost as much for her own benefit as his. 'He isn't old enough to be an avuncular figure like Señor Montañes, and he isn't as young as you are; he's sort of in-between. He was very kind when I was worried about Abuelo, but most often he treats me rather as if I'm a burden he's obliged to bear, and quite naturally I resent it. I object to his being—overbearing and—and arrogant, and I suppose I show it more than I should in the circumstances.'

'So he isn't your favourite person!' Luis sounded as if the idea suited him admirably, and he was smiling. 'Now tell me what Rosa had been up to last night,' he went on, and Kirstie sighed inwardly at the inevitability of it.

'I told you that she saw me in the hall with Miguel one day last week, and I think she'd been waiting for an opportunity like last night. She said she meant to teach me my place, so she rode off with my horse and left me to walk back. Miguel apparently saw her with Scheherazade and when she told him what she'd done for me; although it wasn't the most tactful thing to have done in the circumstances.'

'She's a bitch!' Luis declared vehemently, and when he put an arm around her shoulders his soulful eyes were much less dreamy than malicious. 'I've a good mind not to let her take my gelding out again!'

'You may not need to,' Kirstie remarked ruefully.

'She told me she's going to use Scheherazade, as she isn't really mine.'

Luis pulled a face. 'I don't think she'll get away with that,' he told her. 'Whatever my brother's faults, he's promised you can use the mare whenever you like and he won't let Rosa break his promise.' He eyed her for a moment, then hugged her close in his arm. 'What exactly happened when he came back for you last night, Kirstie?'

'We rode back together, naturally,' she said, studiously casual.

At weekends she spent quite a lot more time with Luis. He expected it and so did her grandfather, for he hadn't relinquished his hopes of a match, no matter how much Kirstie objected to his plans. They had covered almost the entire area of the *patio*, strolling along all the paths and pausing occasionally to sit and talk.

At the moment they were hidden from the house by the bulk of a blue hibiscus, and Luis took both her hands, turning her to face him; his eyes soft and soulful again as he gazed down at her. 'I know it's unlikely in view of what you've told me,' he said, 'but you'd never change your opinion of Miguel to the extent that you'd get to like him *too* much, would you, Kirstie?'

Startled, she stared up at him, and noted with dismay that her heart was beating much too fast and her cheeks were flushed. 'What exactly is that supposed to mean?' she asked.

'It means that I don't want you to do a complete about-turn where Miguel's concerned,' he told her with every appearance of being serious. 'I know it's very unlikely in view of the way you feel about him and the fact that he's so much older than we are, but I couldn't face it if you let him—well, seduce you. He's experienced enough, and——'

'For heaven's sake!' Kirstie interrupted in a breathlessly husky voice. 'You're not being very complimentary either to me or your brother! Miguel will never think of me as anything but a silly little girl who feels more sorry for herself than she has any right to!'

'Ah! That's all I wanted to know.' He slid a hand round under her hair and stroked her neck lightly with his thumb. 'You're so lovely, Kirstie, and I can't help being jealous, even of Miguel. Ever since the first day I saw you I've been dreaming about you; ever since that first moment.'

'Which was not much more than two weeks ago,' Kirstie reminded him gently. She wasn't averse to flirting with Luis, but there was something in his present manner that suggested he wasn't merely flirting.

'Time has nothing to do with it,' he told her. 'Don't you believe in love at first sight, Kirstie?'

'I don't think I do,' she answered cautiously, and Luis frowned.

'I do,' he told her, 'and I'm falling in love with you, Kirstie, whether you believe it's possible or not.'

She was unsure and uneasy. It wouldn't be too difficult, she thought, to fall in love with Luis, because he was good-looking and very attractive and he was undeniably wealthy, which her grandfather considered was another essential quality in a husband. But it was that expressed wish of her grandfather's that deterred her from simply going along with Luis's present mood; it made her suspect her own feelings.

Moving away from him, she half-turned to look at him from a safer distance, then hastily lowered her eyes again, looking for the words she needed. Until she had enlightened Luis she didn't feel she could go on with whatever relationship they already had, and she tried desperately not to make it sound too coldly practical and mercenary.

'Luis——' He came closer and would have taken her hands, but she put out a hand and kept him at a distance. 'I think you ought to know that—my grandfather is anxious for me to marry and he—he thinks you'll make an ideal husband. More than that,' she went on hurriedly when she noticed his look of stunned surprise, 'Miguel seems to be of the same mind, he said once that we'd make a handsome pair. I thought you ought to know.'

'Holy Mother of God!' Hot colour flooded into Luis's handsome features and the soulful eyes were no longer dreamy but snapping with anger. 'What right have they, or anyone else, to organise our lives for us? Holy Mother, I won't *let* them interfere in my affairs; I'll tell Miguel to mind his own business and you'd better do the same with your grandfather! *I* shall choose who and when I marry, and in my own time!' He took her hands again, and his grip was so fierce that she winced. 'Kirstie, is that why you shy away from me? Is it because you've been told I'm an ideal husband and you feel you might be acting as your grandfather wants instead of how you want? Is it, Kirstie?' She didn't answer, but slowly shook her head, and he bent and peered up into her face, his eyes dark and anxious and with only a trace of indignation left. 'Oh, my lovely Kirstie, don't listen to them. I won't pin you down with marriage proposals, please believe me, I won't do anything you don't want me to do.'

'I believe you,' Kirstie told him.

'But I *am* falling in love with you,' Luis insisted, and when she did not answer, he put a hand under her chin and raised her face, looking down at her flushed cheeks and evasive eyes. Then he bent his head and touched his mouth very lightly to hers. 'Do you believe that too?' he murmured.

Kirstie wasn't sure what to believe. She didn't fool herself that she was the first girl Luis had declared himself in love with, for he was the kind of good-looking and wealthy young man to whom love affairs were a way of life. Whether or not he was more serious about her than he had been before, she didn't stop to consider, but she was wary of allowing herself to get too serious about him.

She looked up, smiling a little uncertainly. 'I don't know,' she confessed. 'If you are in love with me, then in a way I wish you hadn't told me, Luis. After only a couple of weeks I can't honestly say how I feel about you, except that I like you a lot, and I like being with you.'

Luis's expressive eyes gazed at her sadly for a moment, then he sighed. 'I'd hoped for something more than that,' he said. 'But it's that damned scheme of your grandfather's and Miguel's——'

'Not Miguel's,' Kirstie hastily corrected him. 'I think he just went along with what my grandfather said, I don't think he really wants it.'

'Well, just forget all that nonsense and act as if the idea had never been put into your head,' Luis advised. He slipped his hands around her waist and drew her close to him, and his eyes glowed darkly as he looked down at her. 'You don't *hate* me, do you, Kirstie?'

'No, of course I don't!'

Her denial was swift, and Luis cut it short when he touched her mouth with his. It was a long, slow and very ardent kiss and it set her pulse hammering much faster than normal, but she had already decided that Luis was experienced with women despite his youth. The only element of surprise was the fact that she was far less affected by it than she expected to be.

When he eventually released her, he looked down at her for a moment and his expression suggested that her response was rather less than he expected too. Putting a hand under her chin, he looked down at her, smiling but puzzled. 'You should be kissed more often,' he decided, and was obviously about to follow his own advice, when Kirstie shook her head.

'Luis, someone might see us out here.'

'So?' He arched an enquiring brow and for a moment looked disturbingly like Miguel. 'Kiss me again, my pigeon, and never mind who sees us or what they say.'

'Luis——'

Next time he kissed her much more passionately so that Kirstie felt a little lightheaded, yet still the magic was missing. And it wasn't because she was worrying about whether or not someone might see them from the house; it was because she remembered too well the way Miguel had kissed her last night. Luis could undeniably touch her emotions, but Miguel's fierce, hard mouth had driven everything else completely from her mind, and she found it infinitely disturbing to realise it.

CHAPTER FIVE

KIRSTIE gazed at her grandfather in blank dismay, her eyes wide and unbelieving. There was a cold sensation in her stomach and for several minutes her brain simply refused to accept what he had just told her. 'I—I just can't believe it,' she said, and sat down heavily in an armchair. 'They wouldn't—they *couldn't*, could they, Abuelo?'

Don José shrugged. He seemed as resigned to this latest turn of events as he had been to all the other changes in his life during the past few months. 'The house and the estate are theirs now, child,' he reminded her quietly, 'and they may do as they like with it. Although you should bear in mind that it's simply a suggestion at the moment, an idea put forward by one of the family, so I understand, but not yet definite by any means.'

'But it's monstrous!' Kirstie declared. Whether or not anything was definite, it was enough that the suggestion had been made. 'They promised, they *promised* that the house was in good hands, and Casa de Rodríguez has always been a private home; for over two hundred years it's been—it was the Rodríguez family home, and now this! A couple of rooms turned into offices I could accept, but not this!'

Her grandfather was looking at her and it was clear from the look in his eyes that he was in sympathy with everything she said—how could he be anything else? But he was so much better at facing the harder facts of reality than she was herself. 'Unfortunately, child,' he told her gently, 'it isn't always enough to want something to be a certain way, it is essential that one's finances keep pace with the outlay, and when that's no longer possible then things have to change, as I know very well.'

'Oh, Abuelo, I'm sorry!' Kirstie was close to tears as she looked at him, but indignation still burned behind the misty blueness of her eyes. 'But that can't be the case with the Montañes,' she insisted, 'they have plenty of money and they don't *need* to do it! They have business interests all over the world and all of them thriving, they don't need any more! They bought Casa de Rodríguez as a home and somewhere to run the estate from, not to turn it into a *paradore*!'

'We really don't know what their original intention was,' Don José pointed out quietly, 'and they already own several hotels, you know.'

'Then they don't need to turn our home into one—they can't!'

'My dear, they can.' He reached and patted her head, but although outwardly he appeared resigned to the inevitable, inwardly Kirstie knew he was as appalled and shocked as she was herself. 'There's no use at all upsetting yourself over it,' Don José went on. 'If it happens we shall just have to accept it as we have everything else that's happened.'

'But I am upset,' Kirstie insisted, and her blue eyes were dark with anguish at the thought of her beloved Casa de Rodríguez being invaded by casual holidaymakers. 'And I have no doubt at all who's behind this—this money-grubbing scheme.' Don José was already shaking his head, instinct telling him where she was placing the blame. 'It's Miguel,' she stated firmly, 'it has to be. It has his mark all over it!'

'Kirstie——'

'I'm right!' Kirstie interrupted him bitterly, and she got to her feet because she simply couldn't go on sitting there any longer, feeling as she did. 'Oh, I know you'll defend him, Abuelo, because you look on him as a friend and he comes to see you, but I don't think you really know him like I do! He can be so—so kind when it suits him, and yet he goes and does something like this; you can't *trust* him!' She shook her head so forcefully that a curtain of black hair swished agitatedly from side to side. 'Oh, I'm going out before I explode! Thank heaven it's a weekend and I don't have to go up there and work with them!'

'Kirstie, please take care, child!'

Her grandfather's warning turned the knife in the wound because it reminded her of how dependent they were on the generosity of the Montañes, and Miguel in particular, for what little they still had, and her sudden laughter was short and bitter. 'Don't worry, Abuelo, I won't tackle Miguel right now, I know what harm that could do! I'm just going for a walk, that's all.'

In fact she had gone no more than a couple of hundred yards before some of her tension disappeared and she felt much less emotional. She regretted upsetting her grandfather with her outburst and when she got back she would tell him how sorry she was, and make him a promise to say nothing to Miguel about it. A promise she would do her best to keep, however difficult it proved to be.

Only when she had thought about it for some time did she recognise the bitterness of disappointment as one of the reasons for her being so upset, and the realisation lurked uneasily in the back of her mind as she walked through the orange groves. Miguel Montañes was a practical man and a forceful one, but this latest proposition concerning the future of Casa de Rodríguez was something she found hard to forgive him for. She felt that in some curious way he had let her down, and it was a disconcerting sensation she did not begin to understand, for he owed her neither loyalty nor explanation.

Since she had come to live permanently in Spain Kirstie wasn't an habitual walker, but at times like this it served to work off her anger, and eventually her thoughts drifted on to other things. Luis occupied a great deal of her free time and she was aware that it pleased her grandfather, though she chose to disregard his reason. What did make her rather uneasy was the way Miguel seemed to watch them whenever they were together. Almost as if he was trying to determine just how far their relationship had progressed, and although she couldn't decide whether he approved or not, she found his interest oddly disturbing.

She was so preoccupied that she nearly tripped over a fallen branch lying in her path, and she bent and picked it up automatically, swinging it in one hand as she went on walking. Fortunately her encounters with Rosa Montañes had been brief and infrequent, but so unpleasant that Kirstie did her best to avoid them.

According to Luis his cousin made no secret of the fact that she did not approve of a young and very attractive secretary coming to the house every day, but so far nothing had been said about changing the situation. And she hoped Rosa Montañes would never attempt to pressure him with that malignant threat of blackmail she had mentioned. Enrique loved his granddaughter.

When she reached the end of the orange grove Kirstie decided it was time to turn back. On foot one's view was much more restricted, but even so it was possible to see some distance in every direction, and it was the sight of something unexpected standing among the twisted grey olive trees across on the other side of the dividing track that caught her eye and made her hesitate, frowning curiously.

She recognised Luis's gelding, a huge and unmistakable brute, but it was the way he stood, riderless and agitated, that drew her attention for as far as she could see there was no other living creature in sight. Even where she stood she could hear the animal's whistling snort of anxiety, and it was that which decided her to go and investigate.

There seemed to be something curiously ominous about the situation that sent little trickles of ice slipping along her spine, and she gripped the broken branch she carried even more tightly as she crossed from one section to the other. Probably it was nothing more than that Luis had dismounted and was checking on something, leaving the gelding to its own devices for a few minutes, but it was the animal's behaviour that made her scalp prickle as she approached it, because it was noticeably anxious.

It shifted its feet restlessly, thudding them alternately on to the dusty earth, and its eyes rolled back as she came nearer, its neck arched and nostrils flared and quivering. Knowing its uncertain temper, Kirstie approached it cautiously, but it seemed almost willing to welcome her and she spoke to it softly and reassuringly, venturing to rub a hand over its sleek neck while she looked around for a sign of its absent rider.

'Suli, good boy.' The rein, she noticed, lay across the saddle and was not trailing as it would have been if the rider had simply dismounted and walked away for a few minutes, and again Kirstie shivered slightly. 'Why are you alone?' she whispered, and the animal pricked up its ears. 'Who was——'

She stopped short and bit hard on her lower lip when she noticed something half concealed by low-growing branches a short distance back from where the gelding stood. It was a moment or two before she could bring herself to walk over there, and when she saw who it was that lay sprawled in the dust her heart gave a sudden jolt of alarm.

Rosa Montañes lay still and inert, and there was a large ugly bruise already discolouring the smooth olive skin of her forehead. She looked so horribly still that Kirstie hesitated to touch her for fear of what she might discover, but eventually a brief and very inexpert examination revealed a slow but steady pulse and a reassuring rise and fall under the thin cotton shirt.

Even so it was essential to get help quickly, and Kirstie wished she had fetched Scheherazade instead of walking. She felt so helpless, for nothing even remotely like this had happened to her before, but she realised that quick action was necessary and that she would have to leave Rosa Montañes where she was while she fetched help.

Shock made her movements slow and clumsy as she

straightened up, and she stood for a second looking down at the woman who made no secret of her hatred for her. It was hard to believe she had been thrown, for she had shown herself to be an excellent horsewoman, whatever her other shortcomings, and yet she lay there bruised and unconscious and looking alarmingly as if she had been hit over the head with something.

It was the unmistakable sound of another rider approaching that made Kirstie look up quickly, and it was quite automatic to offer up a prayer that the newcomer would be Miguel. But it wasn't Miguel, it was Rosa's young daughter, Margarita, mounted on Scheherazade, and the moment she saw her mother's still figure she reined in sharply, her eyes widening in horror, too stunned to move for the moment.

'Mama!' Her voice rose and thinned shrilly, then she looked at Kirstie with a bright glint of panic in her eyes. 'You killed her!' she accused hoarsely. 'You've killed my mother!'

Shock gave Kirstie's eyes a glazed look and she shook her head emphatically as she stared at the girl. 'No,' she whispered. 'Oh no, Margarita!'

Automatically she moved towards her without realising that she still carried the broken branch in her hand, and the girl looked at her wild-eyed with alarm as she came close, her fingers clenched tightly on the rein. More intent on reassuring the girl for the moment than on defending herself, Kirstie too gripped the rein tightly.

'Margarita, your mother isn't dead, she's hurt, that's all, just hurt.'

It wasn't easy to convince her, for the girl seemed incapable of grasping anything beyond the fact that her mother lay ominously still on the ground while Kirstie stood over her with what must look like a pretty formidable weapon in her hand.

'You never liked her,' Margarita accused, her childish voice quivering, and she climbed down off her horse at last, clinging to the animal for a moment before she dropped to her knees beside her mother. 'Mama?' She looked up and her brown eyes shimmered with tears. 'You hit her; you hit her with that stick; you hit her!'

Kirstie was growing desperate, not least because someone had to go for help and Margarita was best equipped, being dressed for riding. 'Listen, Margarita, your mother needs help urgently and you have to ride back to the house and tell your grandfather, or one of your uncles. Get them to call a doctor and an ambulance, do you understand?'

'No!' Margarita crouched over her mother protectively. 'I won't go and leave you with her again, I won't!'

'Margarita, please!'

'No, no, no!'

She was rapidly approaching hysteria, and Kirstie realised there was nothing for it but to go herself as she had originally planned. 'Very well,' she said with a sigh of resignation, 'I'll go.'

But Margarita seemed not to hear. She did not even turn her head to object when Kirstie took Scheherazade instead of the swifter gelding because she felt safer on the mare, riding as she was. Her last sight of the girl was of her small figure kneeling beside her mother in an attitude that was uncomfortably reminiscent of prayer.

It was both inelegant and uncomfortable riding astride dressed in a brief cotton dress, but Kirstie had no time to worry about either as she rode like the wind towards Casa de Rodríguez. Perhaps she had been wrong to leave a young and near-hysterical girl alone with an injured woman, but as she saw it she had had little choice, so no one could blame her.

Nevertheless she heaved a massive sigh of relief when she spotted Miguel the moment she rode into the stable yard, and she called out to him before he could disappear through the gate into the *patio*. 'Miguel, Miguel!'

She didn't stop to consider formalities nor her earlier opinion of him as the desecrator of her old home; he was there when she needed him and she had to admit that she would rather it was him than anyone else. He turned the moment she called to him, and seemed to sense that something was very wrong.

Striding back across the yard, he took note of her dress and reached up to lift her bodily out of the saddle, his big hands almost spanning her waist. Then setting her down in front of him, he regarded her curiously. 'What in heaven's name is the matter?' he demanded, and for a split second when she glanced up at him, Kirstie wondered which of the conflicting stories he was most likely to believe, hers or his young cousin's.

'It's Señora Montañes,' she told him, and her hands were flutteringly unsteady as she smoothed down her rumpled dress. 'She's had a fall from her horse and she's unconscious; she's lying in the first row of olives opposite the track.'

Miguel was already striding through the *patio* gate with Kirstie hurrying breathlessly after him. 'Is she alone?' he asked, and Kirstie shook her head.

'I left Margarita with her; she came along just after I found her mother.'

She didn't mention the girl's opinion of what had happened at that point simply because she wasn't sure how to approach it, and Miguel was swearing as he marched through the gardens with long, urgent strides. 'Damn Luis for being missing when he's needed! Tío Enrique is resting and I don't want to disturb him if I can help it, so I'll have to—No, wait!' He stopped and looked down at Kirstie's anxious face. 'You can ring Dr Sandro and tell him where to find her, and I'll ride down there and see how Margarita is faring. If it's as bad as you say the poor child will be frantic—see to it for me, will you, Kirstie?'

He didn't wait to see whether she agreed or not, but turned and was gone almost before she realised it, leaving her feeling very small and uncertain, for she knew exactly what Margarita was going to tell him when he got there. Hurrying into the house, she made the necessary call for the doctor, but as she walked home along the familiar ride, she couldn't help pondering on the fact that there was a certain irony in the situation. For however reluctant she might be, Rosa Montañes was going to be the one who cleared Kirstie of any suspicion her daughter might arouse.

It was because she told herself that any enquiry from her would be unwelcome by the person most concerned, that Kirstie had not made the effort of asking after Rosa Montañes during the rest of the weekend. She could do so when she returned to work on Monday morning. She didn't like to admit, even to herself, that it was because she lacked the nerve to walk up to the house and ask after the patient, not knowing what kind of a reception she would get.

As it happened she was a little later than usual arriving on Monday morning and rather out of breath as she went hurrying across the *patio*, so that she wasn't sure she wanted to see Miguel. He was leaving the house when she arrived, and he stopped when he saw her, waiting for her to join him.

Standing as he was under the garlands of bougainvillea that draped the overhanging balcony his face was in the shadows and it was difficult to judge what expression was in his eyes as they watched her. But there was a hard line about his mouth that she took heed of, making her heart beat a little more quickly. Only the certainty of her own innocence enabled her to smile faintly as she came up to him.

'Good morning, Don Miguel,' she said, and noted the way one brow arched, presumably because she had reverted to the formality of a title.

'Good morning, Señorita Rodríguez.'

They were both being very formally polite, but there was something in Miguel's manner that rang a warning bell in Kirstie's brain, and she tried to read something in those implacable features that would give her a clue as to how things were. 'I'm afraid I'm rather late——'

'Are you? I'm sure my uncle won't complain about a few minutes.'

Kirstie hesitated. He seemed to have little or nothing to say to her and yet he still remained, looking at her with that disturbingly intent gaze. 'I—I should have asked after Señora Montañes,' she ventured. 'How is she?'

'As well as can be expected—isn't that the phrase?'

He spoke quietly, but something in his voice made her swallow hard, and there was an air about him that made her distinctly uneasy. The niggle of apprehension gnawed again at the back of her mind when she recalled Rosa Montañes lying on the ground and her daughter hurling wild accusations at her. She couldn't really be dead, but if she hadn't come around yet——

'She—She isn't still unconscious?' she asked, and the reply was so obviously important to her that Miguel's eyes narrowed slightly.

'She had recovered consciousness before the doctor arrived,' he said. 'In fact she was coming round when I got there, although she was still confused; and Margarita was babbling away about what had happened.' Kirstie made no attempt to disguise her relief, and again Miguel looked at her narrow-eyed. 'You sound very relieved.'

'I am,' she admitted readily. 'After the way Margarita was talking, I thought you might have——' She shrugged uneasily. 'Well, you *might* have believed her.'

'And is there any reason for me not to?' Miguel asked quietly.

Kirstie stared at him, stunned suddenly and unprepared for a turn of events she could not have foreseen. 'But she was making wild accusations about me having hit her mother with a stick I was carrying,' she said. 'I was stunned at the time, and scared, I don't mind admitting it, but then I realised that the moment Señora Montañes came round she would put her right. Surely—surely she told you what really happened, didn't she?'

'So she's assured us,' Miguel agreed, and Kirstie had seldom heard him sound so pedantic before. 'It more or less coincides with what Margarita told me.'

Staring at him in blank dismay, Kirstie knew that most of the colour had left her face and she felt oddly stiff and cold. 'But—she couldn't! How could she——'

'According to Rosa you lost your temper and hit her with the stick you said you were holding; the one Margarita said you were still holding when she arrived on the scene.' His eyes held hers steadily and, although she found it hard to believe, the hard line of his mouth seemed to have softened a little. 'Would you like to tell me your version?'

Too stunned to take it in properly, Kirstie shook her head. 'It simply isn't possible! I could understand the girl making all those wild accusations, she was frightened and she jumped to the wrong conclusion, but how could—how could Señora Montañes tell such lies? How could she——'

She couldn't go on, but looked at Miguel with eyes that were shocked and bewildered. 'Quite easily, if she wanted to make things uncomfortable for you,' he remarked, and she shook her head because she was convinced it was Rosa's version he believed. 'At the moment it's a case of your story against hers, and of course, Margarita's.'

'So of course you all believe them!' Her lip trembled and a haze of tears gave a shimmering blueness to her eyes as she looked up at him, not knowing why his doubt should trouble her more than any other. 'You believe I'm capable of deliberately attacking someone, maybe killing her, if her daughter is to be believed! You think I'm capable of that!'

'Did I say so?' He slid a hand beneath her chin and raised her pale and anxious face, his dark eyes scanning her features narrowly. 'You judge as hastily as you accuse me of doing,' he told her. 'I know you're an emotional and quick-tempered little creature, and that you've reason enough to dislike Rosa, but to actually attack her?——'

If only he had firmly denied that he believed it, Kirstie would have been content, but his seeming doubt was more than she could bear. It was the second time she had felt let down by him within a very short time, and she turned on him furiously when she recalled the first instance. Jerking her head aside to avoid his hand under her chin, she tossed back her hair.

'I'm not really surprised; anyone who could think of turning Casa de Rodríguez into a *paradore* is capable of believing anything!' she told him bitterly, and swallowed the first choking tears before she could go on. 'And as I'm under suspicion as a possible murderess I'm sure you none of you want me working here, so I'd better go home!'

'Kirstie!'

There was a note in his voice that Kirstie found hard to ignore, but she refused to listen to any more. If he really believed her guilty then it was more than likely the rest of the family did too, and she walked away from him with her back stiff and tears rolling unchecked down her cheeks.

'And don't worry,' she called back in a choked little voice, 'I shan't run away—I'll be around when the *guardia* come for me! Where else would I go?'

She had never in her life felt so miserable or so ill-used as she did when she made her way through the garden towards the gate, and she brushed an impatient hand across her eyes when Miguel called after her. 'Kirstie, stop talking nonsense and come back!'

Kirstie ignored him, although her legs were so unsteady that she didn't know how she managed to walk so determinedly on. It was, she had to admit to herself, not entirely unexpected when the familiar heavy tread of booted feet came after her, and she automatically increased her pace.

Nevertheless Miguel caught up with her well before she got as far as the gate, and his fingers closed around her wrist, bringing her to a standstill, even though she struggled against him. 'Keep still!' he said sharply. 'Don't be such a little fool, Kirstie!'

'Let me go!'

A kind of panic was churning away in her stomach as she fought him, and she was breathing hard and noisily when he eventually put both his hands on her shoulders and swung her round to face him. They were both of them breathing much more rapidly than usual, and there was a curious sense of excitement about the situation that she did not understand at all.

'You're going to listen to what I have to say,' he insisted in an unfamiliarly husky voice. 'Don't behave as if you've been tried and condemned——'

'I have according to you!'

'Nothing of the sort!' She tried once more to brush the tears from her eyes so that she could see him better, and she thought she had never seen him look more dark and menacing. Even so his voice was quiet and well controlled, with just that trace of huskiness, and it was in sharp contrast to the burning intensity she saw in his eyes. He must have felt her relax slightly after a moment or two, for he eased his grip a little and looked directly into her eyes. 'Are you going to listen?' he asked.

'I don't seem to have much option!'

'You haven't!' he retorted, then sighed after a moment or two and shook his head. Then his thumbs slid upward and moved with sensual slowness over the soft skin of her throat, and she shivered in spite of herself. 'I can promise you that nothing is likely to come of this. Tío Enrique doesn't find it as easy to argue with Rosa as forthrightly as I know he'd like to——'

'Because she'd threaten to take Margarita away for good if he did,' Kirstie observed, and he narrowed his eyes slightly.

'Then you know how much he has to lose. I don't think you'll find him very much different from what he's always been, just a little more—wary. Don't make it any harder for him, Kirstie, please; go in as usual, he'll be grateful if you do. The sooner this is allowed to die down the better.'

It was what she had intended doing, but that was

before there was any question of Rosa Montañes not
clearing her, and she hesitated. 'I—I don't know if I
can,' she said, but Miguel wasn't content with that.

He squeezed his hard fingers into her shoulders and
held her firm. 'Of course you can,' he insisted quietly.
'One thing you've never lacked is courage, and unless
you want to give everyone the impression that you're
afraid to face them, you must go in as usual, Kirstie,
hmm?'

His logic was unarguable, and yet it wasn't going to
be easy at all. 'I'll try, if you say so,' she told him with
unexpected meekness, and Miguel's faint smile remarked
on it.

'If I say so?'

'It makes some sense,' she admitted. 'After all, I
haven't anything to hide for, I haven't done anything
wrong whatever any of you think. I didn't touch Señora
Montañes except to help her, so why should I feel guilty
about it?'

'Good!' Once more his fingers pressed into her shoulders and he let his thumbs slide up to stroke the side of
her neck with a light evocative touch that made her
shiver. 'Now—there was another matter you mentioned
that interests me. You said something about Casa de
Rodríguez being turned into a *paradore*? Did Luis tell
you about that?'

It wasn't a subject that Kirstie could discuss easily,
and particularly not so soon after being told with shattering frankness that Rosa Montañes had blamed her
for her injuries, and she looked at him reproachfully.
'Abuelo told me,' she said, and found it irresistible to
add, 'and I told him I didn't need to ask whose idea it
was.'

'You assumed it was me?' He didn't give her the opportunity to answer, but nodded grimly. 'Yes, of course,
you would. Anything that happens that you don't agree
with you automatically attribute to me, don't you, Kirstie?'

'Not without reason,' Kirstie insisted, though not

very happily. If only she had not been so impulsive and broken her promise to her grandfather not to voice her suspicion to Miguel. 'I can't believe your uncle would think up a scheme like that, and Luis— well, who could think of Luis ever turning a beautiful home like Casa de Rodríguez into a one-night stand for passing tourists?'

'Whereas you consider me capable of just about any dirty trick you can think of!' Miguel suggested harshly, and Kirstie stirred uneasily in his grasp. 'Isn't that it, Kirstie?'

Kirstie didn't reply at once. She didn't like the idea of him being responsible, she had to admit it, but in her mind there seemed no alternative. It would have been easier to blame him if only she didn't so easily recall his gentle concern when her grandfather was missing, and the thrill of being in his arms and of being kissed as she had never been kissed before. Now it made her much too unhappy.

'I—I don't know who else to blame,' she confessed in a very small voice, and he sighed deeply as he lifted her face and fixed that disturbingly intent gaze on her again.

'I'm sorry about that,' he said very softly. 'Very sorry indeed.'

Kirstie raised her eyes briefly, alarmed by the rapid and breathtaking beat of her heart. 'I hadn't meant to say anything to you,' she confessed. 'I promised Abuelo I wouldn't, because we owe you——'

'You owe me nothing!' He cut her off with a harshness that she flinched from, and the blazing fierceness of his eyes made her catch her breath. Then he took his hands from her shoulders and ran one of them through his hair, turning back to her swiftly, as if something had just occurred to him. 'Have you mentioned this to Luis?' he asked, and she shook her head. 'Because you just can't believe he'd do such a thing, eh?'

'I don't believe he could.'

'And you hope to marry him, of course.'

Kirstie's colour flared, and she shook her head until her hair swung back and forth across her face. 'That was Abuelo's idea, not mine,' she told him. 'I told Luis about it, and he was furious.'

'Oh?' Miguel looked as if he found it hard to believe. 'Then Luis is a bigger fool than I took him for, and I can't imagine why you—warned him.'

'That you and Abuelo were trying to marry us off?' She shook her head again. 'It was a kind of self-defence. I didn't want Luis to think I had marriage in mind any more than he had.'

'I see.'

Something she saw in his eyes was oddly disturbing so that she glanced hastily at her watch as she sought to change the subject. 'Don't you think that if I'm going to work this morning, I'd better go?' she suggested. 'If you're sure it's all right.' He gave her arm a slight squeeze as he slid a hand under her elbow and steered her back towards the house, and they were already approaching the shadowy cool verandah when she spoke again in a quick anxious voice that sought to clear away the last doubts about the welcome she was likely to get. 'Don Miguel, I hope your uncle *does* believe I had nothing to do with Señora Montañes' accident.'

'He does.'

She glanced up at him, driven on by some irresistible need to ask. 'And you?'

They came to a halt once more just under the overhanging balcony, and Miguel turned her slowly round to face him. 'You may not believe it,' he said softly, 'but I've spent most of the weekend talking Rosa out of sending for the *guardia*.'

Kirstie looked up at him with startled blue eyes. 'You—you spoke up for me?' He nodded. 'But why?'

'Because I don't believe everything I'm told, O.K.?' She was shaking her head slowly in blank disbelief. 'Is it so hard to accept?' he asked.

'I—I just don't know how to thank you.' She looked up and caught something in his eyes that made her heart race like a hammer beat, and it was completely on impulse that she reached up suddenly and brushed her lips on the firm warmth of his mouth. 'Thank you,' she whispered.

After that she would have slipped away, for her own reactions alarmed and surprised her, but before she could move Miguel had reached out and stopped her, drawing her back and into his arms. Just for a moment she was held fast to the lean excitement of his body while his mouth took possession of hers in a kiss that was hard and passionate but disappointingly brief. And she scarcely believed it when he put her from him.

'Go and do some work,' he told her very quietly. 'And if you need someone to blame for you being late, then blame me.'

He was on his way round to the stable before Kirstie recovered sufficiently to realise just how late in fact she was, and as she turned and went into the house she lightly touched her mouth with her fingertips. It was becoming increasingly hard to accept the less gentle aspects of Miguel's character, and she wished with all her heart that she could believe Luis or Enrique responsible for the plan to turn Casa de Rodríguez into a hotel.

Enrique Montañes said nothing at all about his daughter-in-law's accident, in fact his manner was little different from normal except that he was a little more formal than he usually was, and less inclined to make casual conversation. Kirstie would have been happier knowing that he believed in her innocence, but knowing his situation with Rosa she didn't add to his discomfort by saying anything.

Luis's opinion, on the other hand, was equally uncertain but much more easy to ask for. When she returned early from lunch, hoping to make up some of the time lost in the morning, he was waiting for her, and no explanation was likely to deter him. Luis wasn't a man who was easily put aside, so she agreed to talk with him for a short while, and walked along one of the paths with him.

Before long he stopped and took both her hands in his, raising each hand in turn to his lips and kissing her fingers. 'You poor darling,' he sympathised, and kissed her cheek. 'What *has* been going on?'

Resigned for the moment to losing some of the time she was trying to make up, Kirstie shrugged. 'I suppose you mean the business with your cousin,' she said, and Luis clasped her hands even more tightly. 'I was staggered when Miguel told me she was telling the same tale as Margarita, but he informed me there was nothing to worry about because he'd talked her out of sending for the *guardia*.'

'Yes, so I heard,' Luis mused, and pulled thoughtfully at his full lower lip. 'I'm rather surprised to find Miguel championing you though I have to admit, if I didn't know my big brother, my pigeon, I'd be jealous. As it is you look such a little, defenceless creature that he probably feels he has to protect you; especially as he got you the job with Tío Enrique and brought you into Rosa's poisonous sphere.'

'No one in his right mind would believe I'd do anything like that,' she said, 'but it was a relief to know he believed me.'

'It was only what she deserved,' Luis declared with a vehemence that was very much at odds with his usual romantic image, so that Kirstie wondered if he too actually disliked his cousin's widow, and wasn't just saying it for effect. 'I never could stand her, and the way she treats you—I couldn't blame you for hitting her on the head.'

'But I didn't!' Kirstie gazed at him uneasily, for his attitude suggested that he wasn't so much convinced of her innocence, as ready to support her if she really had attacked Rosa. 'Luis, you surely don't believe I did it, do you?'

It was an appeal that anyone would have found hard

to resist, and Luis kissed her long and lingeringly before he answered. 'Lovely Kirstie,' he said, 'it's a matter of complete indifference to me whether you hit Rosa or not.'

Shocked by his callousness towards his cousin as well as by his indifference to her own guilt or innocence, Kirstie pulled herself free and looked up at him reproachfully. 'It isn't to me,' she told him. 'And at least Miguel had enough faith in me to talk Rosa out of having me arrested!'

Luis's pursed lip suggested he disliked losing on comparison with Miguel. 'Or else he doesn't want a scandal,' he suggested with a hint of malice in his soft voice. 'Miguel is very conscious of our family dignity, and he'd hate it if we made the headlines in an attempted murder case. He'd talk anybody out of anything to prevent that.'

He couldn't mean it, Kirstie told herself, and yet there was an awful cold, sick feeling in her stomach as she stood there facing him. Miguel hadn't actually told her that he believed her version, not in so many words. Then she remembered the touch of his lips, and his kiss seemed suddenly to have the bitterness of a kiss of Judas.

'Would he—would he really think about that?' she asked in a very small voice, and Luis seemed completely unaware of her reaction.

He shrugged his eloquent shoulders carelessly. 'Who knows how Miguel's mind works?' he said. 'He has a touch of Machiavelli about him sometimes, and none of us can follow his machinations. All we know is that he puts the family first and always; you can depend on it, my love.'

'Machiavelli!' Kirstie echoed bitterly. 'Yes, that just about says it, doesn't it?' He was looking at her curiously, and impulse drove her on. 'I shan't easily forgive him for suggesting that Casa de Rodríguez should be turned into a *paradore*—that's a typically Machiavellian move!'

Luis's velvet dark eyes were narrowed briefly when they met hers, then they switched to her mouth and stayed there while he pursed his lips thoughtfully. 'I didn't know that idea was general knowledge,' he remarked, and it was impossible to guess what his own opinion was. 'How did you come to hear of it, Kirstie?'

'Abuelo told me, and he almost certainly got it from Miguel; I suppose he saw no reason not to boast about it, he probably thinks it's a brilliant idea!'

Luis pondered for a moment, then he leaned and kissed her mouth, drawing her close so that the warmth of his body touched her through the thin dress she wore, and the somewhat over-sweet after-shave he used made her wrinkle her nose for a moment. 'Would it be the unforgivable sin to make Casa de Rodríguez into a *paradore*?' he wanted to know, and to Kirstie the wonder was that he needed to ask.

Pushing herself away from him, she still remained in his arms, but she could see his face and try to judge how serious he was. 'I didn't think you'd need to ask,' she told him, 'you know how I feel about it, Luis. I know I lived there for only seven years, full-time, but the Rodríguez go back a long way and I suppose the feeling I have is bred in me. I hate to think of strangers sleeping in its rooms for a couple of nights and then passing on to the next—novelty. It's a home, it's always been a private home, it isn't a showplace for tourists, and I think Miguel was—insensitive and—and unfeeling to even suggest it!'

It still hurt; surprisingly so in the circumstances, and Kirstie fought hard not to let him see how embarrassingly weepy she was feeling. But Luis seemed preoccupied still, tracing a finger down her neck and on to the curve of her shoulder. 'Did he admit it was his idea?' he asked, and Kirstie frowned at him, seeing it as splitting hairs.

'Not in so many words, but he didn't deny it either, and who else *could* it have been? I know it couldn't be you or your uncle, so it had to be Miguel.'

'The Philistine of the family?' he suggested, and laughed shortly. 'Poor old Miguel!'

She was uneasy, sensing something she didn't understand, something in his manner that did not seem in accord with her own mood, and it occurred to her that he might resent her talking about his brother as she did. 'I'm sorry, Luis, I shouldn't say things to you about him, he is your brother after all.' A glance at her wristwatch offered a way of escape and she pulled a wry face before she made her excuses. 'I must go, Luis. I was very late this morning and I want to make up some of the time if I can. Señor Montañes is very nice about it, but I don't want to take advantage of it.' Raising her head just far enough, she planted a kiss on his chin, then smiled up at him, though it wasn't a smile that reached her eyes and she thought he noticed it. 'One thing, I'm glad it wasn't you being so horribly mercenary; I'd hate to think I was such a bad judge of character. *Adios*, Luis!'

But instead of letting her go, Luis pulled her back and into his arms, kissing her mouth lightly, over and over again until she was breathless, and that was what Miguel saw when he came along a few moments later. The minute she caught sight of him, Kirstie pushed Luis away with both hands and the colour was high in her cheeks. She wanted to feel defiant and uncaring, to let him see that he wasn't the only man who kissed her, but instead she felt small and oddly weepy again because of what Luis had told her.

For the moment he ignored her and tapped Luis on the shoulder, making him turn swiftly in surprise. 'I'm sorry to interrupt,' he said smoothly, 'but we have a lot of riding to do this afternoon and it's time we got started.'

'I'm ready when you are,' Luis told him, and gave Kirstie a curiously shifty look that didn't fit in with his image at all.

'The trouble is, you *weren't* ready when I was,' Miguel argued abruptly. 'While you were dallying out here with

Kirstie I've spent the last ten or fifteen minutes waiting around for you. Is your horse saddled and ready to go, or do I have to wait until you do that too?'

His arrogance was no less with members of his own family, and Kirstie was in complete sympathy with Luis when he flushed like a scolded schoolboy, his eyes gleaming darkly with resentment. 'Don't talk down to me, Miguel,' he told him sharply. 'I dislike it! It won't take me more than a minute or two to saddle the gelding and I'll be ready!'

He gave Kirstie a brief salute, then went stalking off with his head held high and the stiffness of anger in his stride, obviously expecting Miguel to follow him. Instead Miguel stood looking down at Kirstie in that vaguely menacing way she had become familiar with during the past months. 'Have you been coping?' he asked, and she angled her chin.

'Perfectly, thank you!' She was haughty as much on Luis's behalf as her own, but haughtiness never paid off with Miguel, and his eyes narrowed slightly.

'Then I suggest you go back to the office as soon as possible,' he suggested coolly, 'before my uncle has a change of mind!'

He was already turned and walking away from her when Kirstie called after him. 'Do you object to Luis kissing me?' she challenged, and Miguel stopped and turned back slowly.

His eyes gleamed below heavy lids and he tapped the long quirt he always used on the palm of one hand as he looked at her. 'Why should you think that?' he enquired softly. 'I know how much you enjoy being kissed.'

His meaning was unmistakable and Kirstie coloured furiously as she hastily avoided his eyes. It was much easier to remember the steely embrace of his arms and the hard passion of his mouth than it was to recall Luis's kiss of only a few moments ago, and her heart thudded so hard that it filled her head with its beat. Then she turned quickly and went hurrying across the *patio*. No one, but no one, should affect her as Miguel did, and especially when she tried so hard to dislike him; when she had so much reason to dislike him.

CHAPTER SIX

KIRSTIE had seldom felt so low in spirit before, and inevitably her grandfather noticed and remarked on it. 'I'm all right, Abuelo,' she told him, but the old man was shaking his head.

'There's nothing wrong at the house, is there?' he insisted, and Kirstie knew she must have given herself away when she so quickly gave her attention to her sewing again. 'What is it, child?' he pressed gently. 'It has nothing to do with that unpleasant business with Señora Mantañes has it? I was under the impression that Don Miguel had settled that to your satisfaction.'

'He seems to have settled it to someone's satisfaction,' said Kirstie. 'At least no one has said anything more about it to me.'

'Then what *is* wrong, child?' He reached and lightly patted her hand. 'Is it anything to do with your—relationship with Luis Montañes?'

Kirstie had grown accustomed to that delicate pause, but she still frowned over it, for she knew that her grandfather put quite a different interpretation on that relationship than she did. 'It has nothing to do with Luis,' she assured him.

'Ah, good!' His obvious satisfaction irritated her too, because no matter what she said to him, her grandfather would not yield an inch on the desirability of a match between her and Luis. 'You make a very handsome couple, my dear, and I'm glad to see you getting along so well.'

'Luis and I are good friends, Abuelo, but that's all. We're neither of us thinking of marriage at the moment; in fact Luis was as indignant as I was about the idea when I told him what you had in mind for us.'

'My dear child!' Don José looked shocked as Kirstie expected he would. 'How on earth could you bring yourself to discuss such a thing with him?'

'Because it concerns Luis and me more than it does anyone else,' she told him with a defiance she rarely used to her grandfather. 'And I told him before Miguel did. There was some kind of misunderstanding where Miguel was concerned,' she went on to explain. 'He said one day that he thought I should be married and naturally I thought you must have mentioned your idea to him; I know how you talk together. I didn't realise it was sheer coincidence, but once he knew what you had in mind he immediately guessed you'd thought of Luis.'

'It's all most unethical,' Don José declared, but for all that Kirstie could see he was interested in Miguel's reaction. 'Did he seem in favour of the idea?' he asked.

Kirstie, who had long since despaired of guessing what was going on behind that dark enigma that was Miguel's face, shrugged uneasily. 'Who knows what goes on in Miguel's mind? Even his own brother accuses him of having a Machiavellian streak, and I have to agree; you never know just where you are with him.'

She noticed a catch in her voice and realised that she was finding it increasingly hard lately to mention anything to do with Miguel without getting her emotions involved. And her grandfather, she realised, was shrewd enough to notice it if she wasn't very careful. 'Do you still dislike him so much?' he asked, as if he found it very hard to understand.

'I mistrust him,' said Kirstie, and again noticed that her voice wavered slightly.

'But surely after he went to so much trouble to persuade his cousin not to pursue that ridiculous allegation, you must realise how much he has your welfare at heart, child.'

Her grandfather had heard only her first rosy-tinted view of Miguel's efforts, she had never mentioned Luis's alternative, or how much it had troubled her for nearly a week. It was a quite incomprehensible hurt that niggled away at the back of her mind, and she had vowed not to let it bother her so much, but no matter how she tried it still hurt because almost certainly he had not made his plea for her sake alone.

'It—it's not at all certain that he settled it for my benefit, Abuelo,' she told him, and her grandfather frowned at her curiously. 'I thought at first that he had talked Señora Mantañes out of calling the *guardia* because he was convinced of my innocence, but it seems more than likely I was wrong. Luis suggested a more practical possibility. He—he says Miguel was more likely to have been concerned with preventing a public scandal that involved members of his family.'

Don José seemed to accept the possibility much more matter-of-factly. 'It's very possible,' he mused. 'Naturally he's concerned with the good name of his family, but that's not to say he isn't convinced of your innocence too, my dear.'

Kirstie hadn't been able to accept it as coolly; she only knew that Miguel had disappointed her for the second time within a few days, and it rankled. Her hands were clenched tightly and she found it hard to believe that she was close to tears as she went on, 'He made me think—I—I thought he was telling me that he knew I couldn't have done it, but when Luis pointed out the more likely explanation I—I realised that he'd never actually said he believed me, I just assumed it.' She clasped her hands tightly over the sewing she had on her lap and laughed a little wildly. 'I should have known better than to take Miguel for granted, after all only a few days before that I learned that he'd had the bright idea of turning Casa de Rodríguez into a tourist attraction! It's so difficult to know what to make of him. One minute he seems so kind and—and caring, and the next——' She shrugged helplessly.

Her grandfather was watching her closely and there was a gentleness in his eyes that would have been her undoing if Kirstie had looked at him. 'My dear child,' he said softly, 'is that what's making you so unhappy?'

'Not unhappy,' Kirstie insisted hastily, 'just angry. I don't enjoy being made a fool of, and Miguel Montañes seems very adept at doing just that!' She put aside her sewing and got up, brushing her hands down her dress with anxious fluttering movements while she spoke. 'Oh well, one day I suppose I'll learn not to take him at face value! If you don't mind, Abuelo, I'd like to go for a ride and get rid of some of the cobwebs. I won't be gone very long.'

'Are you going alone?' Don José asked, but Kirstie pretended not to hear him, and closed the door firmly behind her.

Although on Saturdays Luis most often went with her there were occasions when he was unable to be there because he had been given something else to do. Usually by Miguel, who seemed never to have heard of the five-day week. It seemed this was one of the occasions, for she noticed that both the stallion and Luis's gelding were missing from their stalls, but she shrugged as she saddled the mare, for she was nothing loath to be alone in her present mood.

In fact she hadn't ridden for a day or two because she simply hadn't had the time, and she thought it might have been as well in case she saw Rosa Montañes. They seldom met during working hours, but as they both rode there was always the possibility of them bumping into one another, and she knew the other woman was fully recovered because Luis had told her so. He had also bemoaned the fact that she seemed in no hurry to go home.

It often intrigued Kirstie that of the two brothers Margarita seemed to favour Miguel, for it seemed a curious choice when Luis's more romantic image would seem to have more appeal for a young girl. Miguel for his part seemed to have a special affection for the girl, and it occurred to Kirstie that he might possibly be more attracted to his cousin's widow than he allowed anyone to know. Very possibly his affection for the girl grew naturally from his feeling for her mother. Tall, sophisticated and thirtyish, Rose Montañes possessed all the necessary attributes that Luis claimed were what his brother looked for in a woman.

She rode at a leisurely pace through the orange groves and found the space and peace of the *huerta* as soothing as always, thoroughly content with her own company. A little whitewashed *barraca* squatted beside the track on her right, and as she approached it a woman appeared in the gateway, making it appear very much as if she had been lying in wait for her.

She stood watching with small black eyes until she came up level, then she showed broken yellow teeth in what Kirstie presumed was meant as a smile. 'Good afternoon, Señorita Rodríguez! A fine day for riding.'

Kirstie smiled automatically. She had no idea who the woman was, for she had never had any dealings with the estate workers, but the woman obviously recognised her and courtesy was habitual in this country. 'Good afternoon, *señora.*'

No more was required of her, but a certain look in the woman's sharp black eyes made her uneasy and she would have urged the mare on if the woman hadn't spoken again. 'Are you well, *señorita*? You and the *señor*?'

On the surface it sounded like common civility, and yet there was something more than that behind the enquiry, Kirstie was convinced. If she had not pulled up, the mare would have carried her by before she could answer, so she reluctantly reined the animal to a halt. 'We're both very well, thank you, *señora*—and you?'

A slight nod confirmed her own state of health. 'It's sad you're no longer at the house where you belong,' the woman remarked, and now, Kirstie thought, they were coming to the point. 'When Don José was master life was better for all of us!' Her jet black eyes were narrowed, judging the effect she was having on her listener. 'Don José wouldn't have put me out of my *barraca*, he left folk in peace, but this one——' The gesture she made suggested that she would have spat but for present company. 'Out by the end of this month, he says, and the month almost up! Blessed Holy Mother, but he's a devil, that one; a devil, *señorita*, as you will know to your cost!'

Kirstie had no doubt at all that she was referring to Miguel, but her own resentment of the opinion surprised her momentarily. She wasn't really prepared to lend an ear to a tale of injustice, but it was doubtful if she was going to be given the opportunity to avoid it, so she sighed inwardly and dismounted.

It seemed to be taken for granted that she would follow the woman through the gateway and into a wretchedly overgrown little *patio*, but she did so very reluctantly. 'I'm afraid I know nothing about estate business, *señora*,' she said, making her position clear from the start. 'I—we have nothing to do with it now.'

'That's as maybe,' the woman allowed, and tapped a finger against her prominent nose, leering in a way that brought colour to Kirstie's cheeks. 'But you ride with one of them often, I've seen you. And with *him* too a couple of times, though you didn't look as if you were enjoying it very much—who would? The other one now, the young one, he makes you smile.'

The last thing Kirstie wanted was a discussion about her relationship with Luis, and she was shaking her head, making ready to leave again. 'I don't know what it is you want to say to me, *señora*,' she said in an attempt to move from more personal subjects, 'but I haven't much time.'

'Just spare me a moment,' the woman insisted, and her black eyes watched her closely. There was something distinctly unpleasant about her and she made Kirstie restless and anxious to be off. 'It's easy to see you have the ear of one of them at least, *señorita*, and if you was to say the word to the young one I might not have to go at the end of the month.' She regarded her slyly, showing another glimpse of broken teeth. 'You couldn't refuse to help me could you, *señorita*, knowing how it feels to be put out of your house?'

The allusion to the loss of Kirstie's own home brought a flush of resentment, but it also caught her sympathy, for she could remember only too well how it felt. 'I—I don't know,' she demurred, shaking her head. 'I don't think anything I say would have much effect, *señora*.'

'But you could *try*!'

Kirstie shook her head slowly, weighing up the chances of success. 'I really don't think I could do anything, *señora*,' she said. 'Although I do sympathise, and I know exactly how you must be feeling.'

'But it might not do your own chances any good, eh?' Kirstie frowned at her confusedly and the woman jeered. 'Oh, you've seen the best way to get your own house back, and don't think I blame you, even if you won't help me. Either of those two fine *caballeros* would take you for his wife, you're pretty and you're young, and don't say it hasn't occurred to you! I dare say even that heartless devil who's throwing me out of my house could fancy a pretty piece like you, and he's older and got more say I dare say. But me—hah! What chance do I have of marrying a rich man to get my house back?'

Kirstie turned swiftly and walked in a daze back through the open gateway, and only then did the woman realise how she had over-played her hand. Short thick fingers grasped her arm anxiously and the voice had a placatory whine as she hurried along after her. '*Señorita*, for the love of Holy Mary!'

She *did* know how it felt, and despite her anger Kirstie found herself unable to refuse the plea. It would have to be Enrique she approached, for she refused to ask anything of Miguel, and Luis did not have the necessary authority. Taking the mare's rein, ready to mount, she turned and looked at the woman over her shoulder.

'I can't promise anything,' she said in as firm a voice as she could muster, 'but I'll have a word with Señor Montañes, the senior partner. If you tell me your name——'

'Josefa Medina,' the woman supplied hastily, and Kirstie nodded as she swung herself up into the saddle.

'I'll see what I can do,' she promised.

'Heaven bless you, Señorita Rodríguez!' The sharp black eyes glowed in triumph. 'And heaven send a soft heart to that devil so that he marries you and gives you your home back!' Her cackling laughter followed Kirstie as she jabbed her heels hard into Scheherazade's flanks, and brought fresh colour to her cheeks.

She could not even guess what Enrique was likely to say when she approached him and she was already regetting her promise. There was probably a very good reason why the wretched woman had been given notice to quit, and if he did anything at all he would consult with Miguel about it first; for the estate workers came under Miguel's jurisdiction.

She was getting close to home when she spotted two other riders coming along the track at right angles to her and closing fast. At first glance she assumed it to be Luis and Miguel, but it didn't take long to realise that it wasn't Luis riding the gelding but Rosa Montañes. Obviously being thrown by the animal had not deterred her from taking it out again, and Kirstie had to admire her courage if nothing else.

She realised she had been seen and recognised in turn when Miguel raised a casual hand in greeting, and from the way he turned his head it could have been that he suggested putting on some speed to join her. Already ruing the bad luck that had brought Rosa across her path again, Kirstie took quick action to avoid an actual meeting.

There was a chance that if she could goad a turn of speed out of the mare she had a chance of beating them back to the stable and being unsaddled and gone before they put in an appearance. It was worth a try, she decided, and put her heels sharply to the surprised mare, who took off like the wind. Had Miguel been alone it was quite possible he would have given chase as he had

done on one occasion, but the presence of Rosa Montañes would put paid to any chance of that happening
in this instance.

She had in fact got the mare unsaddled and finished
rubbing her down before she heard the other two horses
come into the yard, and the deep, husky sound of Rosa's
laughter brought a tightness to her mouth that was
completely involuntary. She heard the scrape of
booted feet on the stone sets in the yard and then the
flinty clop of hooves coming across to the stable, and
she turned the corner into the doorway, only to be
brought up sharply by the tall figure of Miguel block-
ing her way.

He was leading both horses, and between one raised
arm and a horse's shoulder she saw Rosa Montañes
swinging jauntily across to the *patio* gateway. Kirstie
stepped back quickly, her heart hammering wildly and
her head seeming so light suddenly she couldn't think
clearly. Miguel smelled of horses and leather and that
very special masculine scent that always hung about
him, and it was very hard indeed to remember that
she had told her grandfather how untrustworthy he
was.

Also there was a look in his eyes that ran little shivers
up and down her spine as he regarded her steadily. 'Are
you still running away?' he asked, and Kirstie blinked
at him in bewilderment, forgetting that that was exactly
what she had done by making the effort to get back
first and avoid a meeting with his companion. 'You were
very obviously running away when you saw us just now,'
he stated confidently. 'Rosa realised it and it gave her a
great deal of satisfaction.'

'Did you really expect me to wait for you?' Kirstie
asked in small voice. 'I thought it was more discreet if I
avoided a meeting in view of her opinion of me. I would
have thought even you understood that!'

He took note of the inference with a raised brow,
but made no other comment for the moment. Instead
he led the two animals into the building and put each

into its own stall, leaving the stallion while he attended to the more restless gelding, and it was automatic for Kirstie to linger in the doorway and watch him.

She always took so much more detailed notice of Miguel than she did Luis and nothing escaped her watching eyes as she studied him. A cream shirt stretched tautly across his broad back when he bent to undo the girth and showed the shadow of dark skin through its texture, and the deftness of his big hands reminded her of how gentle they could be at times, and at others so thrillingly and excitingly sensual. She knew it was dangerous, thinking about Miguel like that, but somehow she couldn't help herself. Whatever he did, however he behaved towards her, Miguel fascinated her in a way no other man did.

'Didn't I see you leaving one of the *barracas*?' he asked, so suddenly that it took her a moment or two to bring herself back to earth.

Apart from anything else, he was the last person she wanted to discuss their vengeful tenant with, and neither was she happy about his questioning her visit. 'I did call on someone briefly,' she allowed, but he still didn't turn his head and look at her.

'Any reason why you chose that particular woman to visit?' he wanted to know, and she frowned.

'I hadn't much choice, as it happened,' she told him, 'she seemed to be lying in wait for me. But I didn't realise I needed permission to visit one of the tenants, Don Miguel; I'm sorry if I broke one of your rules!'

He turned briefly and looked at her over one shoulder as he lifted off the gelding's saddle, and it was much more difficult to meet his eyes than she would have believed. 'Don't be clever with me, Kirstie.' He spoke quietly, but there was a dark gleam in his eyes that resented her sarcasm. 'I'm rather surprised you have anything in common with a woman like Josefa Medina, that's all.'

'I have one thing at least,' she told him. 'We both know what it's like to lose our homes!' She stared at the broad, unresponsive back and quite forgot that she had decided to speak to his uncle rather than say anything to him. 'She says you've given her notice to leave her cottage, poor woman. I didn't like her much, but it seems very hard to be put out of her home.'

'You think we should go on housing a thief?'

The condemnation was so harshly said that she felt a shiver flutter along her spine for a moment. Then she recalled his having once told her that he had been obliged to dismiss one of the women for stealing, and how annoyed he had been at her reaction. It seemed he still saw her as condoning the woman's dishonesty.

'You told me about a woman you'd dismissed for stealing,' she said in a rather small voice. 'Is she the one?' Miguel nodded without turning or speaking, and Kirstie shifted uneasily. 'I—I didn't know that when I promised to do what I could for her.'

'And who were you going to ask for help, Kirstie?'

The quietness of his voice stirred alarming responses in her, and she moistened her lips anxiously before she answered him. 'Señor Montañes,' she said, then spoke up hastily in her own defence because she knew how he would blame her for not making him her object of appeal. 'He *is* the senior partner.'

'And you'd rather go to the devil himself than ask me for anything, wouldn't you, Kirstie?'

He still didn't turn and look at her, but the gelding's glossy coat flinched from the hard strokes of the hay-wisp, and she could see how tightly he held it. Her heart was thudding urgently and her eyes had a darkly defensive look as she watched him, but she couldn't let herself be beguiled again, not when she knew how bitterly he could disappoint her.

'It—it seemed like the logical thing to do,' she murmured, both hands clasped around the edge of the wooden partition and her cheek resting on her hands. 'Señor Montañes is my employer, after all.'

Miguel ignored her, giving his whole attention to the gelding, and the strained silence eventually became unbearable. The logical thing to have done would have been to leave him and go back to the house, but somehow she couldn't bring herself to do that, and instead stood watching him, her mouth pursed reproachfully.

Then the stallion on the other side of the partition stamped his feet and snorted impatiently, tired of waiting his turn, and Kirstie reacted with the same impulsiveness she so often did. 'I might as well take care of Hassan,' she said. 'At least I can get his saddle off.'

'No, Kirstie, leave it!'

The warning was so brusque and authoritative that just for a moment Kirstie heeded it instinctively, and stopped just around the corner of the partition. But there was no reason why she couldn't cope, for she had been taking tack on and off horses for most of her life, and although the stallion was a bit bigger than average there was no reason why she couldn't lift off his saddle.

Presumably Miguel had assumed she would obey, for after a moment or two of listening silence she again heard the hay-wisp in action and slipped alongside the stallion in his stall. Undoing the buckle of the girth-strap was easy, but reaching up to take off the saddle, she discovered, required more height than she had, and it was heavy. She might have got away with it even so, if the animal hadn't shifted suddenly in his impatience and put her off balance. With a cry of surprise she fell forward and landed face down between the horse's feet, with the saddle wedged uncomfortably underneath her.

'Kirstie!' Miguel came round the end of the partition and grabbed her swiftly from between the stallion's restless hooves, then pinned her back against the partition and glared at her with fierce dark eyes. 'In the name of all that's holy, what are you trying to do?' he demanded, and added as an afterthought, 'Are you hurt?' Breathlessly Kirstie shook her head, but he thrust a hand under her chin and forced her head up so that he could look into her face. 'Are you sure?'

'I'm quite sure, thank you.'

Her voice was husky and shivered with uncertainty, but that had as much to do with his being so close as with being pulled around, and as he peered into her face and frowned, his mouth hovered much too close for comfort. 'He could have trampled all over you, do you realise that?' he asked. 'Why didn't you do as I said and leave him to me?'

'I—I don't know.'

Her voice wavered unsteadily and her breast rose and fell with the unevenness of her breathing, and as he leaned towards her his body touched hers with a light evocative touch that almost shattered her self-control. 'I do,' Miguel said softly. 'You just don't like doing as you're told, do you?'

'There's no reason why I should,' Kirstie gasped in a last effort to keep control of the situation, but the pressure of his body holding her against the partition teased her unmercifully and she turned her head to avoid the hand under her chin. 'And I'm quite capable of unsaddling a horse, whether you believe it or not!'

'Not an animal the size and strength of Hassan,' Miguel insisted, and she tried to jerk herself free when he placed his hands on her shoulders and held her firmly. 'Don't let me see you near him again, Kirstie, nor Suli either, they're both too big for you to manage, so stay with something your own size, eh?'

'I was trying to help,' she insisted, and a faint smile touched his mouth for a moment.

'I can manage,' he told her.

'And so could I have done if the silly creature hadn't moved away,' Kirstie retorted. 'And I do wish you'd stop treating me like a sweet, helpless little five-year-old, Don Miguel—I'm getting a little tired of it!'

His fingers pressed into her shoulders hard for a moment until she shrugged in protest and there was a gleam in his eyes that sent shivers all through her body. Still keeping his hold on her, he pulled her away from the proximity of the impatiently snorting stallion and out of the cramped confines of the stall, and she gasped when he pushed her roughly against the stone outer wall and kept her there with the pressure of his body.

His face was so close that every word he spoke breathed warmly against her mouth and teased her senses until she looked up at him in mingled defiance and anticipation. 'Holy Mother,' he declared, 'no one could accuse you of being a *sweet* little anything! You're the most determinedly aggressive female I've ever met, and I'm tempted to sweeten your temper in a way you won't forget; I'm sure your grandfather would thank me for it! Why do you do it? I don't see you behaving like this with my uncle or Luis!'

The heat of his body was like a fire that drew her to it irresistibly until she actually felt the rippling muscles under the skin, and the hard, steady beat of his heart. 'They're—they're different,' she whispered, and widened her eyes in surpise when he laughed suddenly.

'Would they like that?'

His eyes had a faintly mocking and infinitely disturbing look and she shook her head, tossing her long black hair back and forth until it flicked across his face. A strand of it caught on the moistness of his lips and his eyes, heavy-lidded and black as jet, looked down at her steadily as he took the straying wisp and pressed it briefly to his mouth before brushing it back with the rest from her neck.

Sliding his hands around her, he drew her away from the wall and into his arms, and the touch of him kindled such a wild exultant joy in her that it forced a cry from her lips as he swept her against him. Just briefly something stirred in her brain that fought against the wild abandon of her response, but the moment Miguel took her mouth it was forgotten, swept away by the tumult of emotion that consumed her as she lifted her arms to encircle his neck.

The vibrant force of his desire shivered through her and she clung to him, letting herself be swept along, unresisting and eager, burning with the same force that

fired him. Not even the tread of booted feet on the stone
sets outside meant anything for several moments, and
then it was Kirstie who first became aware that they
were no longer alone. She fought for breath to tell
Miguel while he murmured wordless sounds in the muffling softness of her hair.

'Miguel!' The harsh voice and imperious tone could
only belong to Rosa Montañes and as she heard it
Kirstie's heart skipped in sudden panic.

She used both hands to push Miguel away and looked
at the woman standing in the open doorway of the
stable, eyes blazing with fury and her hands tightly
clenched. His hastily assumed calm would have fooled
her if she had not been close enough still to feel the
intensity of passion that still burned in him and made
her tremble, and he put her from him with such obvious
reluctance Rosa could not help but have noticed it.

'Rosa?'

If he intended questioning her reason for being there
Rosa left him in no doubt. She darted quickly forward
and grabbed a handful of Kirstie's hair, tugging vic-
iously hard as she swung her round by it and almost
brought her to her knees. 'Bitch!' she screamed in a
harsh flat voice. 'You murderous, deceitful little
bitch!'

'Rosa, in God's name!'

Miguel gripped both her hands and hung on, a bruis-
ing grip that must have hurt, but which served to make
her let go, and his eyes burned as furiously as Rosa's
did. Recovering slightly, Kirstie stood with both hands
to her tingling scalp, staring in disbelief at the vengeful
woman who now stood gripped in Miguel's relentless
hold.

'Kirstie.' He let go the other woman's hands and
reached for hers, but Kirstie drew back out of reach.

'Please don't!'

How could she have been such a fool as to let herself
become involved in a situation that was bound to have
repercussions one way or another? She had promised

herself it would never happen again, but she had suc-
cumbed as she had done before to the special kind of
power that Miguel seemed to have, and now Rosa
Montañes had even more reason to hate her. At the
moment she found it very hard to think clearly and all
she knew for certain was that she wanted to be as far
away as possible from both of them. If she had need of
proof that what Luis had said was true, Rosa had just
demonstrated it; she meant to marry Miguel and she
would fight tooth and nail to get him, and at the
moment Kirstie didn't feel equal to the contest. She
turned and hurried away, angry, hurt, and tearful.

The story she told her grandfather was a little less than
the truth, for he knew by now how much Rosa Montañes disliked her, but the shock that awaited her on
Monday morning when she reported for work was unexpected. It was Enrique who broke it to her that she
was not to be allowed to visit the stables again and take
out Scheherazade for their customary rides.

'I'm very sorry about it, my dear,' Enrique told her,
and she could not doubt that his regret was genuine. 'I
know how you enjoy your riding, but Miguel agrees
with me that it's for the best while my daughter-in-law
is here. I'm sure you understand.'

'Yes, of course I understand,'

She had made no protest, laid no blame, for she knew
just how much pressure would have been put on Enrique
to get rid of her altogether, and she could only thank
heaven that she at least still had her job. But to be forbidden to see her beloved horse was harsh punishment
indeed, and she burned with resentment at the injustice
of it. She had responded readily enough to Miguel's kiss,
she couldn't deny it, but it had been Miguel who in-
itiated the situation, and now it seemed he was in complete agreement with the decision to ban her from riding
for as long as Rosa Montañes was around.

There was little she felt she could say in her own defence to Enrique, but Miguel was another matter and

she felt her anger and resentment rise again when she saw him the following morning as she arrived for work. He was on his way round to the stable, and that somehow added insult to injury, so that she glowered at him reproachfully from beneath heavy lashes as she came up.

'I'm sorry about your riding,' he told her, 'but Tío Enrique was forced to take some kind of action and he couldn't bring himself to dismiss you from your job.'

'And you were in agreement, of course!' Her indignation swelled to fury at the matter-of-fact way he spoke about it, mostly because it seemed he was to get off scot-free. 'I'm the natural choice for culprit, of course, being the outsider!'

'In God's name,' Miguel exploded wrathfully, 'don't start feeling sorry for yourself again! You surely don't expect me to be banned from riding, do you, you foolish child, I have to get around, it's my job!'

'Don't call me *child*!' Kirstie told him furiously, and for a moment she wondered if he was going to hit her, he looked so angry.

Running one hand through his hair, Kirstie realised he was keeping a very tight rein on his temper, and she wondered for the first time just how much blame he had had to take from his uncle, not to mention Luis. For Rosa, she thought, was unlikely to have kept it to herself. 'I understood from my uncle that you'd accepted the decision without fuss,' he said, and only a slightly rough edge on his voice betrayed how he was feeling. 'He said you were very reasonable about it.'

'You uncle didn't kiss me,' Kirstie declared in a huskily unsteady voice, 'you did! The result is I'm not allowed to take out Scheherazade any more while you can carry on as usual! You said when I came for my interview,' she reminded him,' that I wouldn't have to see you very often, and you don't know how much I wish it was true! I suppose it was because we—we were in the stable your cousin thinks it's our customary meeting place and that's why she's had me banned from riding!'

'Kirstie!'

There was an odd roughness in his voice and his eyes gleamed at her darkly, but Kirstie had suddenly thought of an alternative and she couldn't resist letting him know it. 'Fortunately,' she went on, 'you only own two of the horses; Suli belongs to Luis and I don't think he'll deny me the use of him if I ask him nicely.'

'God in heaven,' Miguel breathed harshly, 'you'll do no such thing, you little fool, that damned gelding would break your neck! And if Luis has no more sense than to let you talk him round I'll see he's sorry for it, and you can tell him that! I'm sorry about your riding, but you and Rosa are far more likely to meet around the stable or when you're riding. You've seen what Rosa is capable of, so take my advice and keep out of her way, Kirstie, or I can't answer for the consequences; I may not be around the next time and you could *really* get hurt. I know you're not very good at accepting the inevitable, but in this instance try and be sensible about it.'

So as far as he was concerned it was all cut and dried, but he hadn't once mentioned his own part in the incident leading to the ban, and that infuriated her. 'I shall ask Luis to let me have Suli,' she told him, her chin set stubbornly, 'and if you don't want me going round to the stable then Luis can meet me somewhere else. I presume there's no ban on Luis riding your horses, so he can take Scheherazade.'

'Damn you, Kirstie, will you see reason and do as I say? Rosa can manage the gelding because she has stronger hands, she's stronger altogether than you are, but for God's sake stay away from him.'

Instead of answering, Kirstie turned and walked towards the house feeling him watching her every inch of the way, her legs oddly unsteady when she considered her triumph. Luis wouldn't deny her the use of his horse; he'd never liked Rosa much anyway and they didn't have to meet in the stable. She heard the hard tread of booted feet walking away as she went into the house, but she didn't turn and look, only wondered why she felt so much like crying suddenly.

CHAPTER SEVEN

IT was nearly a week since Kirstie had been able to ride and she missed it even more than she realised she would. She was very disappointed in Luis too, for his expected readiness to let her ride the gelding in defiance of the ban had not materialised, and although he would probably deny it indignantly, she suspected the reason was because he was fearful of deliberately crossing Miguel.

When he heard of the cause of the ban, initially he had behaved very much like a jealous *novio*, and for a man who had declared he had no intention of marrying her it wasn't the reaction she looked for. She hoped she had eventually convinced him that the kiss Rosa Montañes had made so much fuss about was nothing like as important as her jealousy made it seem. But still there was a brooding dislike in Luis's dark eyes sometimes when they rested on her, that suggested a small doubt might still linger.

It was because there was less likelihood of their being interrupted that Luis had come down to the *barraca* during the long lunch break to see her, and although there was less space to lose themselves in, the little *patio* garden was lush enough to provide privacy. Her grandfather was unlikely to put in an appearance because he still nurtured the hope of a match between them, and there was no chance of Miguel coming upon them.

Their conversation was along the inevitable lines, and in the circumstances Kirstie supposed Luis was very patient. 'Apart from anything else,' he told her as they sat together on a wooden bench just inside the *patio* gate, 'there's the risk, Kirstie; Suli's a brute and he's no respecter of persons.'

Never one to let go easily, Kirstie persisted. 'But Rosa still rides him,' she pointed out, to which Luis's reply was dismayingly similar to Miguel's.

'Rosa is quite different from you. She's stronger and bigger altogether; Suli would toss away a little creature like you and never even notice it.'

Luis kissed her cheek lightly, then turned her towards him and sought her mouth, but Kirstie had other things in mind and her response was absent. 'You're sure you're not simply afraid of what Miguel will say?' she suggested, and knew she had hit the nail on the head when she saw the way he reacted.

His head jerked up swiftly and his eyes gleamed with resentment, for he had the Spanish male's traditional sensitivity when his courage was questioned. 'I'm afraid of no one!' he informed her, and Kirstie took him up on it at once.

'Then let me have Suli!'

He got to his feet, looking very much like Miguel as he stood there for a moment regarding her steadily and with a trace of exasperation in his eyes. But when she got to her feet as well, he sighed and took her face between his two hands, leaning towards her so that his mouth was tantalisingly close, and his voice was low and slightly husky. 'Why do you plague me so about that damned brute?' he asked. 'Is it just so that you can get the better of Miguel?'

'Partly.' Kirstie admitted it with a breathless little laugh. 'Although he'd more than likely heave a great sigh of relief if Suli did break my neck, because I'd be out of his hair once and for all.'

As if she had meant it seriously, Luis considered the suggestion gravely for a moment, then shook his head. 'Miguel doesn't kiss girls he doesn't like, and from the way Rosa described it, Miguel wasn't simply giving you a kindly kiss of consolation this time.' He was frowning again and there was a small flutter of reaction in Kirstie's heart that was infinitely disturbing. 'I'd like to know exactly what *did* happen, Kirstie; I don't like the situation any more than Rosa does, to be honest, and I can't help thinking——' His dark dreamy eyes had a certain glint of shrewdness so that Kirstie lowered her own gaze rather than look at him. 'Had it happened before, Kirstie? I mean, have there been other times, apart from that time in the hall when your grandfather was missing?'

Because it was easier to think clearly if she wasn't in touch with him, Kirstie eased herself away and walked a little way along the narrow path. A pointless manoeuvre since Luis followed her closely. She was tempted to deny that there had been other occasions, but she had a feeling that he wouldn't believe her.

'A couple of times,' she admitted casually, as if it was easy to dismiss kisses that had seared her heart and soul with their fierceness, 'but I'm not silly enough to take them seriously, even if Señora Montañes does.'

'I see.' And he did, she thought, despite her attempt to make light of it, for he suddenly beat one fist into the palm of his hand and he was scowling in a way that quite spoiled his good looks. 'Damn Miguel,' he swore, 'why can't he leave you alone? What gives him the right to kiss you where and when he feels like it? I don't like it; you're my girl, not his, and he has no right!'

'I'm no one's,' Kirstie insisted firmly, but there was a slight flush in her cheeks and a gleam in her eyes that Luis took note of as he again took her face in his hands and gazed down at her.

'You're not in love with him?'

'In *love* with him?' Until that moment it hadn't even crossed her mind, but it occurred to her suddenly just how close she had come on one or two occasions to falling in love with Miguel. It was an alarming and a disturbing thought and she hastened to put it away from her, shifting her gaze to avoid Luis's dark, brooding eyes. 'I'm not in love with anyone,' she told him. 'No one at all.'

'Oh, surely a little with me, my pigeon, eh?'

'I could be, I suppose.' Pressing her face between his hands, Luis frowned over her reluctance to admit it, but Kirstie looked up at him again suddenly and she pursed her mouth reproachfully as she sought to bring the con-

versation back into safer channels. 'But obviously you're
not wholehearted about being in love with me or you'd
lend me Suli!'

Luis groaned as he ran both hands through his hair
and shook his head slowly. 'I can't risk him throwing
you as he did Rosa, please understand that, Kirstie! And
I didn't come here to spend my time talking about my
wretched horse!'

He attempted to draw her closer, but something he
had said had caught her attention, and Kirstie held him
off, looking up at him curiously. 'You said—throw me
like he did Rosa,' she reminded him. 'The last time we
spoke about that you were prepared to believe I'd hit
her and knocked her out; are you convinced now that
Suli threw her?'

'I'm convinced!' Luis agreed impatiently, and attempted to pull her close again. 'I know now that's what
happened. Kirstie!'

He pulled her close against him and kissed her much
less gently than before, holding her so tightly that she
could scarcely breathe, let alone move, and just briefly
the significance of what he had said faded from her mind
as she was carried along with his passion. From her
mouth, his lips moved on to her half-closed eyelids, to
her neck, and the soft pulsing spot at the base of her
throat, until eventually the increasing ardour in his
voice, muffled in the thickness of her hair, and his hands
roused her to realisation, and she turned her head swiftly
from side to side.

'No, Luis!'

In the soft confusion of her hair, his voice was ragged
with emotion. 'I'll do anything for you, my love,' he
vowed recklessly. 'If you want Suli I'll give him to you—
he's yours!'

'Oh no, Luis!' Anxiously she pushed him away, looking up into his handsome and slightly flushed face with
dark glowing eyes that were so disturbingly like Miguel's
at the moment that she shivered. 'I don't want your
horse; I couldn't take him. Miguel would never forgive

ither of us if you did anything as silly as that!'

'Miguel!' He pulled her breathtakingly tight into his
rms again and spoke close to her ear in a thick hoarse
oice. 'Miguel has too much to say about things, it seems
o me! If you don't want to have Suli, you can at least
ide him, my pigeon!' He eased her away for a moment
nd looked down into her slightly bemused eyes, smiling
nd defiant. 'I shall be there to make sure nothing hap-
ens to you, so why not? Does that please you, hah?'

'Oh, Luis!'

On impulse she tiptoed and kissed him, and Luis
ulled her close again to kiss her mouth with a hard
rgency that took her breath away. 'And you'll remember how I have indulged you, won't you?' he whis-
ered.

Quite sure that he would remind her if she ever did
orget, Kirstie nodded. 'Can we go this evening?' she
entured, and his immediate reaction was a frown that
uggested he was already beginning to regret having
een so impulsive.

'You won't waste any time, will you?' he asked, and
vas obviously considering it carefully. 'It won't be easy
nd I shall have to be careful about bringing out two
orses together, in case Miguel sees me.' He thought
bout it for a moment, then nodded slowly. 'I'll bring
uli down here before Miguel gets back and then take
cheherazade afterwards, at the last minute. If he notices
hat Suli is gone he'll think either Rosa or I have taken
im, and if I can get the mare out without him knowing,
o much the better.'

'That sounds O.K.'

In fact Kirstie felt surprisingly badly about deceiving
Miguel, but she wouldn't let Luis see it, and he looked
own at her with bright speculative eyes for a moment,
hen kissed her mouth lightly and smiled. 'We can get
he better of Miguel between us, my lovely, eh?' Kirstie
odded. 'I'll come for you about seven?'

'About seven,' she agreed, but there was a slightly
eflective look in her eyes that he noticed and ques-

tioned. 'I was thinking about what you said earlier,' she
told him. 'You said you knew now what had happened
about Rosa being thrown. What exactly did you mean
Luis?'

Luis shrugged, and it was clearly not the subject he
had in mind to discuss, but Kirstie was looking at him
in a way that suggested she was not interested in anything else at the moment. 'Miguel got the truth out of
her,' he said. 'He finally got her to admit that Suli bolted
with her and she was knocked off her seat by a branch
across the track. She admitted that you'd had nothing
to do with it at all, that she hadn't even seen you.'

'Just as I said.'

It was odd how strangely humbled she felt suddenly.
She had so readily accepted Luis's alternative suggestion
that Miguel's only motive in persuading Rosa not to
call in the *guardia* had been to prevent a family scandal.
The fact that he had gone to the trouble of making her
tell the full truth could only mean that he had done so
with the specific purpose of clearing Kirstie of blame.

'Rosa didn't want to admit it,' Luis went on, and
clearly he wasn't altogether happy about his brother's
motive for exerting so much pressure, 'but Miguel
worked on her like a latter-day inquisition.'

'I'm grateful to him,' said Kirstie, and felt a wonderful
sense of satisfaction, even though Rosa Montañes was
likely to hate her even more because of it.

'It's cleared the air, I suppose,' Luis allowed grudgingly. 'Rosa would never have allowed anyone but
Miguel to talk to her the way he did, but you know
Miguel when he puts his mind to something, he never
lets go.'

'I know,' Kirstie said softly, and wished suddenly that
she had the nerve to tell Luis she would rather not ride
his Suli after all.

It had seemed such a long day to Kirstie, and the fact
that she had seen nothing of Miguel seemed to matter
far more than it usually did. Now that she knew how

determinedly he had prised the truth out of Rosa it somehow made the prospect of her clandestine ride with Luis rather less enjoyable, and she wished she knew a way to tell Luis that she'd had second thoughts. It would give rise to endless speculation if she suggested it, and she couldn't face Luis's inevitable questions.

With one eye on the time, she was putting the finishing touches to the evening meal that would be ready for when she came back, and she could feel her grandfather watching her, making her uneasy. The kitchen and the tiny *salón* were connected by an open archway and it was easy to carry on a conversation with someone in the next room, although so far her grandfather had said nothing of what was on his mind.

Lunchtime was the first time Luis had called at their home and Don José had been delighted to see him, although it was clear that he had expected to be given more of his time than the mere formality of an introduction and a polite request that he speak with Kirstie alone for a few moments. Kirstie had realised it, but not Luis, and she was half expecting the matter to be raised sooner or later.

'I hoped when Don Luis came here today that he came with a specific purpose in mind,' her grandfather observed, and Kirstie sighed inwardly because she knew exactly what specific purpose he was referring to.

'He came to talk to me, Abuelo, that's all.'

A raised brow made it plain that Don José suspected her of being evasive. 'From the short time I was able to see you in the garden,' he said, 'that young man came for considerably more than polite conversation, Kirstie. In view of the way he was behaving then I quite expected him to ask to talk to *me*; he's a very—demonstrative young man. Has there been any mention of marriage between you yet?'

'None,' Kirstie replied promptly. 'I'm afraid you're going to be disappointed if you expect Luis to propose, Abuelo, he isn't ready to marry anyone yet, and I strongly suspect it won't be me he settles on when he is.'

'Then he has no right to behave as I saw him behaving at lunchtime!' Don José declared firmly, and Kirstie left what she was doing and came through into the *salón*, smiling and shaking her head.

'Oh, that doesn't mean a thing to Luis; not to anyone these days, Abuelo.'

Don José looked distinctly shocked and it startled Kirstie to realise just how much her grandfather still lived in the world of his youth, yet she couldn't find it in her heart to blame him. 'No young woman should take her reputation so lightly,' he admonished, 'not even these days, my child. I'm quite certain that neither Señor Montañes nor Don Miguel would countenance such behaviour in Don Luis if they knew of it.'

Kirstie's pulse was beating so much harder suddenly, and she kept her eyes downcast, watching the fingertip that traced a pattern on the arm of her grandfather's chair. 'I can't answer for Señor Montañes,' she told him, 'but Don Miguel is fully aware of the way Luis behaves.'

'And he doesn't object?' Don José demanded. 'I find that very difficult to believe, Kirstie!'

Kirstie knew he had a very soft spot for the man who had, she was forced to recognise, done all he could to make her grandfather's loss as bearable as possible, and she hesitated to shed a different light on him. Yet it was because they were so friendly and Miguel had not mentioned his own occasional lapses in that direction that she wanted to correct his picture of him. Miguel had his good points, she had good reason to know that, but he was not the paragon of virtue that her grandfather saw him as; a view that in Kirstie's opinion made him appear less of a flesh and blood man than he really was.

'Don Miguel is in no position to object, Abuelo,' she told him quietly, 'because he's kissed me himself on more than one occasion. The last time was when Señora Montañes saw us together in the stable one day last week; she made such a fuss about it that I've been forbidden to visit the stables again or to ride Scheherazade, until she's gone home.'

'My dear child!'

'So now you know why I haven't been riding for nearly a week,' Kirstie said, and her grandfather frowned at her curiously, not yet taking in the full significance of what she had said.

'Don Miguel has forbidden you?'

Kirstie shrugged. 'He and Señor Montañes agreed it between them, I think. Rosa Montañes can be pretty nasty, in fact I know she once threatened to keep Margarita away from her grandfather if she couldn't get her own way.'

'A very unpleasant character,' Don José observed disapprovingly.

'Very, but as it happens I am going to get a ride if Luis can bring off the plan he has. He's finally agreed to risk Miguel's wrath and let me ride Suli.'

'Surely if you've been forbidden——' Don José began, but she shook her head quickly.

'Suli doesn't belong to Miguel as the other two horses do, and he's worked it out that if he can bring Suli out and then sneak Scheherazade out for himself we shan't actually be breaking any bans. Except that Miguel has threatened Luis with all kinds of retribution if he lets me ride the gelding. Anyway, it's done now.'

She shrugged because she was less and less happy about the whole idea, although she would have to go through with it now. The way her grandfather was looking at her did nothing to make her feel any better either. 'You're proposing to go riding despite the ban on your doing so?' he asked, and Kirstie nodded.

'Providing there are no hitches, Luis should be here about seven for me, so he said.'

Don José was silent for a moment, then he got to his feet and he was drawn up to his full height as he looked at her so that Kirstie instinctively shrank from the wrath to come. Her grandfather could look every inch the proud *hidalgo* when he chose to, and his features were implacable, leaving his feelings in no doubt.

'Whether or not there was good reason for Señora Montañes' jealousy I won't go into now,' he told her, 'but I know Don Miguel as a good and generous man. Your plan to deceive him, quite deliberately, is underhand and quite unworthy of you, Kirstie. Riding is a privilege granted to you by Don Miguel and it shows a sad lack of gratitude on your part when you set out to deceive him! When Don Luis comes you will——'

'It's too late,' Kirstie told him, and her own regrets added weight to her grandfather's criticism. 'The gelding is already tethered just outside our *patio* wall, Abuelo, and Luis will here here in a few minutes.'

'Kirstie!'

'I know, I *know*!' She turned and looked at him and her eyes were suspiciously misty. 'I wish I could get out of it now, especially since Luis told me how—how Miguel forced Rosa to tell the truth about her accident, and cleared me of blame. But what can I do?'

Don José regarded her steadily for a moment, then he shook his head slowly. 'It seems Don Miguel has your welfare very much at heart,' he observed quietly. 'Which makes your deceiving him very much worse, my child, don't you agree?' Kirstie nodded miserably. 'Therefore when Don Luis arrives either you will tell him that you want no part of the deception or I shall tell him myself.'

Kirstie bit her lower lip anxiously, for she knew how Luis was going to react whichever one of them told him the ride was off. 'I—I'll tell him,' she promised in a small husky voice. 'I don't know how I'll tell him because I've begged him and begged him for nearly a week to let me ride Suli, his gelding, against Miguel's strict instructions, and if I tell him I've changed my mind——'

'Isn't it possible he'll be relieved?' her grandfather suggested quietly, and Kirstie had to admit to the possibility.

'Perhaps,' she allowed with an unhappy shrug.

Her grandfather was a stern and authoritative man, but he was also a loving one, and she was so obviously contrite that he was moved to take her in his embrace and pat her shoulders consolingly. 'You're a foolish child,' he murmured, 'a pretty, foolish child, and I can only hope that you find a strong and loving husband to care for you. Now that I've learned more about young Don Luis I'm not nearly so certain he would make a desirable husband for you, he's far too irresponsible.'

Kirstie could not restrain a smile, and she kissed him fondly. 'I've known that all along,' she told him, 'but you were so keen on the idea, Abuelo.'

A brief nod acknowledged his error, but Don José looked thoughtful as he glanced at his wristwatch. 'As you won't be changing into riding clothes,' he said, 'change into another dress, Kirstie, that one is far too businesslike for having dinner. If Don Luis comes while you're changing I'll entertain him until you're ready; that is if you're certain you want to tell him yourself about your change of plan.'

'I'm certain,' Kirstie told him, and hugged him for a moment. 'Thank you, Abuelo.'

The little *barraca* was built all on one level and it had taken her a long time to get used to everything being so close together; in truth she still wasn't really used to it. Going into her bedroom simply meant walking from the tiny *salón* through another door leading from it, and she heard her grandfather heave a great sigh as she closed her bedroom door. He really had set great store by Luis as a husband, she thought, but it had never really been even a remote possibility; she liked Luis, she found him very attractive, but she didn't love him and that was the only reason she would marry any man, rich or poor.

She had washed and changed her dress and was brushing her hair when she heard a knock on the outer door. A hard, brief knock that for some strange reason set her pulse racing wildly, and had her staring at her bedroom door in a kind of dazed curiosity. It could be Luis, it *should* be Luis, and yet every instinct told her that it wasn't.

The buzz of voices followed as her grandfather admitted the caller, and the moment she heard the other man's voice, even muffled as it was by the thick wooden door, she knew she had been right. What concerned her most was why Miguel was there instead of Luis, for she couldn't quite believe in the coincidence of them both calling at the same time, and she stood for several minutes with the hairbrush held tightly in one hand.

She couldn't hear what was being said, just the two voices talking together, and the frustration of not knowing was nerve-racking. The suspense ended when a light tap on her door preceded her grandfather's quiet but authoritative voice. 'Kirstie, if you're dressed will you come out here, please?'

She didn't reply, but put down the hairbrush and opened the bedroom door. Only her grandfather was visible at first, but when he turned and walked back across the *salón* she saw Miguel standing by the window, so tall that he seemed to fill the little room with his presence.

Dressed as she most often saw him, in slim-fitting light trousers and an open-necked shirt, with the bottoms of the trousers tucked into short leather boots, he was an impressive figure by any standard. And with his broad shoulders pulled back and a dark, menacing look in his eyes when he turned around from the window, he made her feel very small.

His mood was conveyed by the steady tapping of a red leather quirt against one leg, and she eyed it warily. 'Don Miguel.'

He inclined his head in a very formal bow, and it was hard to believe he had held her in his arms and kissed her such a short time ago, for his formality froze her with its chill. She glanced at her grandfather appealingly, but he seemed not to notice, and she wondered just what the two of them had been saying before she came out of her room.

'I have Don José's permission to speak with you alone for a few moments,' said Miguel, and it went without saying that her grandfather had given his permission without hesitation, she thought.

'Abuelo?'

Don José looked at her and shook his head; his eyes were gentle but his manner was unrelenting. 'It's a reasonable request, child,' he told her quietly. 'Don Miguel has something he wishes to say to you, and while he does so I shall sit in my bedroom.'

'Please, that won't be necessary, *señor*,' Miguel assured him, respectful as always to the older man. 'If Señorita Rodríguez will come out on to the *patio* with me——'

What else could she do but agree? Kirstie thought as she nodded consent. Her grandfather was just as much aware of what Miguel was there for as she was herself, and obviously he was going to let her handle the interview as she had said she wanted to. Only then she had been anticipating talking to Luis, not Miguel.

Outside, the scent of oranges was sweet and heady, and Kirstie made directly for the shade of the only tree their tiny *patio* possessed. She stood under the spread of its branches feeling as she had never felt in her life before, and finding it impossible to decide whether it was anxiety alone that made her heart race the way it did. The way Miguel affected her had always been cause for concern, and it was especially so in the present circumstances.

He stood facing her, and he looked so menacingly dark in the shadows, so gloweringly stern, that she found herself shaking like a leaf. For several moments he did no more than stand and look at her, and eventually the silence became so unbearable that she turned and moved off a pace or two, clasping her hands together in front of her. She spoke in a soft halting voice that must have told him exactly how she was feeling.

Luis's plan had obviously gone wrong and she felt guilty about her own part in it for his sake, because it had been her insistence that had made him do it. She had no doubt he had already felt the full weight of

Miguel's wrath, and now it was her turn; Miguel was too shrewd to attribute the entire blame to his brother.

'I—I was expecting Luis.'

'So I understand,' said Miguel, and something in his voice was as hard as the look in his eyes, sending shivers coursing along her spine like a flurry of icicles. 'Need I say he won't be bringing the mare down here?'

She looked over her shoulder at the open archway into the grove automatically. 'Where—where is he?'

It didn't really make any difference, she thought hazily; Luis would be somewhere nursing his pride, and it would soon be her turn to do the same, if that dark ominous gaze was any guide. 'You'd better consider your own position instead of worrying about my brother,' Miguel told her harshly. 'I'm not exonerating Luis, but I can guess just how much pressure was put on him before he agreed to that stupid trick. He'd promised me that whatever happened he wouldn't let you ride that damned gelding, and I think he would have kept his promise in normal circumstances.'

Kirstie had never seen him in this mood before and there was a harshness about him that touched unexpected depths in her. She was ready to admit her responsibility, but alarmed at the possible outcome once she had admitted it, and she passed a moistening tongue over her lips first. 'I—it was my fault basically, I kept asking Luis to let me ride Suli and——'

'And what did you eventually offer him that he found too hard to resist?' he demanded. 'Or am I being indiscreet, Señorita Rodríguez?'

It took a second or two for Kirstie to realise the full import of what he said, and when she did she stared at him in disbelief, the colour burning in her cheeks. And yet in some strange way it hurt much more than it made her angry, and she didn't begin to try and understand that. 'You have no grounds—you have no—no reason to say anything like that,' she whispered, shaking her head slowly back and forth. 'Luis wouldn't—he had no possible cause to say anything like that.'

'I know Luis,' Miguel told her in the same flat, cold voice. 'He'd have to have some very strong inducement to take the risk of causing a family quarrel, and you're defiant and wilful enough to promise anything as long as you get your own way!'

'No!' She was desperate to convince him and alarmingly close to tears; still more hurt than angry, although her emotions were so tangled it was difficult to know exactly what she felt. 'You—you don't know me at all if you can think—what you're thinking, and I thought——'

'I know that you've never been ready to accept the inevitable,' Miguel insisted relentlessly, 'but this time you're going to, or by God you're going to be sorry!'

'You can't——' she began, but he cut her short ruthlessly.

'I can do whatever I think fit,' he told her, 'and somehow or other you're going to have to learn that you can't go your own sweet way whatever the circumstances!'

He hadn't mentioned the fact, but on more than one occasion her grandfather had reminded her how dependent they were on the good will of the Montañes, and she looked up at him anxiously. 'You wouldn't—you wouldn't put us out?' she ventured, and told herself she couldn't believe it of him even in this toweringly angry mood.

For a long moment Miguel said nothing, but the quirt still tapped against his boot and the glowing blackness of his eyes burned her like fire. 'Your opinion of me never changes, does it?' he asked. 'I have too much respect for Don José and, I hope, too much humanity to put you both out of your home, but your own position——'

He didn't finish the sentence, but he had no need to, and Kirstie hadn't meant to let him see how close to tears she was. Now it was too late for there was nothing she could do to stop them and she hastily used her fingertips to brush them away. 'Is Señor Montañes going to dismiss me?' she ventured in such a small voice that it was barely audible, and for a moment Miguel regarded her narrowly, almost as if he suspected her of trying to play on his sympathy.

'So far no one knows about this but you and Luis and myself, and Don José, I understand. You should be thankful that Rosa knows nothing or my uncle would have had no choice this time but to get rid of you. You stay away from the stables and the horses, is that clear?'

'Yes.'

'And you do not pressure Luis into lending you the gelding.' She nodded, brushing the tears away with her fingertips again. 'Give me your word that you won't indulge in any more stupid tricks like this and no one else *need* know.'

'I promise!' She wondered how far he would believe her now, but his manner had softened slightly, she thought as she looked up at him from the thickness of her lashes. 'I—I'd already promised Abuelo that I'd tell Luis when he came that I'd changed my mind.'

'I know, Don José told me.' Yet he had still turned the full fury of his anger on her, Kirstie thought hazily, and again brushed at her misty eyes. Miguel took a large white handkerchief from a pocket and thrust it into her hand. 'Dry your eyes,' he instructed in a voice that was much more like normal.

With the handkerchief to her eyes, she used its cover to look up at him. 'I changed my mind about going when Luis told me about Rosa—Señora Montañes,' she told him.

'I haven't the remotest idea what you're talking about,' Miguel informed her brusquely, but although he professed ignorance Kirstie believed he knew perfectly well what she referred to.

'I'm talking about the fact that you—worked on your cousin until she told the truth about the attack I'm supposed to have made on her,' Kirstie insisted, and hurried on when he looked as if he might interrupt. 'Luis told me how you made her tell what really happened, and it was such a relief to know that you really did believe my version after all.'

'Believe you?' He frowned at her curiously. 'Of course I believed you, you little fool. However many short-comings you might have, I don't count attempted murder among them.' He eyed her narrowly for a moment. 'What other possible reason could you think I had for persuading Rosa not to call in the *guardia* right at the beginning?' he demanded, and Kirstie shrugged uneasily. 'Well?'

She hesitated, carefully avoiding his eyes while she tried to explain how she had been prepared to believe he was more interested in guarding his family's name than in clearing hers. 'You—you could have been con-cerned with preventing a scandal,' she said.

'Luis's suggestion?'

He was shrewd enough to see his brother's hand behind it, and Kirstie saw little point in denying it.

'But Abuelo said it was a reasonable thing for you to be more concerned with your family's good name,' she told him, and glanced up at him again briefly. 'Of course Abuelo approves of almost anything you do.'

'Unlike his granddaughter!' The quirt was laid across the palm of his other hand and no longer tapped im-patiently, but while he spoke he poked with a booted foot at the edge of the flower border. 'I understand that Don José disapproves of the way Luis behaves with you, taking into account the fact that Luis has made it quite clear he isn't going to marry you.' He turned and looked directly at her, and his eyes were slightly narrowed and questioning. 'Do you have any complaints about the way Luis behaves, Kirstie?'

It wasn't an easy question to answer in the circum-stances, and her heart was beating alarmingly hard and fast. Keeping her eyes downcast, she hoped she sounded unsurprised by the fact that he had been discussing her affairs with her grandfather. 'I've nothing to complain about,' she told him, her voice slightly husky. 'Luis does—take things for granted sometimes, but as I've told Abuelo, that's the way things are these days, it doesn't have to be taken too seriously and I can cope. He—he was so sure Luis was going to marry me, although I'd told him from the start that he wouldn't.'

'You don't want to marry Luis?'

It seemed scarcely credible that she was standing there discussing her relationship with Luis, with Miguel of all people, but the softness that was now in his voice made it hard to take offence and she merely shook her head. 'I'm not as concerned with marriage as Abuelo is. It was a silly, old-fashioned idea to want to marry me off like that, and I told him I wouldn't even consider it.'

Miguel was regarding her with his deep, dark eyes, and little shivers slipped along her spine. 'You never will accept the inevitable, will you, Kirstie?'

'Being forced into marriage isn't inevitable,' she argued.

'Not being forced against your will, I agree,' Miguel conceded quietly, 'but it is inevitable that you'll marry sooner or later, you must realise that, surely.' A hand slipped beneath her chin and he looked down into her face for a long moment, searching every feature as if he sought some indication to her innermost feelings. 'Any man who marries you will need to be very strong-willed,' he went on, still in the same quietly affecting voice. 'You're wilful, disobedient and discontented, and you need a much firmer hand than Luis could provide.'

It was some wild, irresistible impulse that made her react as she did, and the urgency of her heartbeat drove her on. Looking up at him, at the dark, implacable face with its depthless eyes, she met his gaze boldly and directly for a moment. 'Like you?' she suggested huskily, and Miguel's hand tightened about her chin until his fingers dug bruisingly hard into her skin.

Then he bent his head and touched his mouth to hers, just lightly at first, until passion flared suddenly and consumed her. His mouth was hard and fierce, just as she remembered it, and it ravished her senses, while a hand slid down to her throat and the thumb moved in a light, sensual caress over the throbbing pulse at its base.

He held her close, so close that the sheer bold maleness of him touched every nerve in her body, and she responded to it with an abandon she had never known she possessed. Her whole body pulsed with a wild, irresistible desire and it was as if she had left the world for a place so much more thrilling that she had no wish ever to leave it.

When he eventually released her mouth it was very, very slowly and with obvious reluctance, and his lips were pursed slightly to prolong the contact as long as possible. 'You could always get under my skin,' he murmured in a smokily husky voice that was warm against her mouth, and his eyes had the depth and blackness of jet when he looked down at her. 'I believe you'd marry *me*, and I know I could cope with you; also I have it on his own word that Don José would rather have me than Luis!'

Kirstie gazed up at him, her eyes hazy with disbelief for a moment before she shook her head. She recalled the buzz of voices in the *salón*, but not for a moment had it occurred to her what they were discussing, and when the full implication of his words finally came home to her she struggled frantically to be free of him.

It was all too easy to imagine her grandfather, disappointed at Luis's adamant decision not to marry, approaching Miguel instead, and she realised that she was shaking like a leaf. Her breathing was deep and exaggerated and must have shown him exactly how deeply she was affected. She hadn't much to bring him in the way of worldly goods, but she was pretty enough and her pedigree was impeccable, something that would be important to someone like Miguel with his family pride; she imagined it all.

'I'll never forgive him!' she whispered in an agony of humiliation, and the tears ran unchecked down her face. 'How *could* he!'

She broke free of him, half stumbling in her anxiety to get away, and only vaguely heard Miguel's voice as she ran into the house and straight into her own room where she slammed the door behind her. Nothing—but nothing would induce her to go to Casa de Rodríguez ever again, and she certainly couldn't face Miguel again.

CHAPTER EIGHT

IT was the very first time Kirstie had had angry words with her grandfather, and the exchange had proved almost as upsetting as the reason for her anger. Don José had not given her a full explanation, but he had allowed that he and Miguel had discussed the matter of finding her a husband, and that alone had been sufficient to invoke her fury. He acted only with her best interests at heart, her grandfather insisted, and in the circumstances he considered her reaction unreasonable.

'Unreasonable!' Kirstie had echoed bitterly. 'It's enough that you think me incapable of running my own life, but to approach Miguel as you did is the last straw! Can you imagine how he must have been feeling when he spoke to me? No wonder he was angry! And then when we—when he—Oh, I could curl up and die when I think about it! How am I ever going to face any of them again?'

Kirstie couldn't honestly have said that he seemed upset by her tirade, but he was surprised by it, and he had not understood the need to give up her job with Enrique. To Kirstie there was no other course, for whether Miguel mentioned her grandfather's proposal to the rest of his family or not she simply couldn't face the embarrassment of seeing him again, so she made no attempt to go to Casa de Rodríguez the following morning.

She supposed she should have given Enrique some kind of explanation, offered an apology for her absence and given him proper notice of her intention to quit. But they had no telephone and except for going to the house, she had no means of communicating with him. Maybe when she had had time to recover her equilibrium she would call and see Enrique, but at the moment she simply couldn't face any of them.

153

Going for a walk was merely a way of getting away from the cottage and giving herself time to think things over, but she longed for the company of her beloved Scheherazade. The way things were at the moment it seemed very unlikely she would have the opportunity to ride again, and as she set out Kirstie thought how many things had changed for the worse lately. The sense of insecurity that had begun when they had to leave Casa de Rodríguez seemed overwhelming suddenly, and her eyes filled with tears as she walked along the track between the orange trees.

The irrigation channels that poured life into the fertile *huerta* did not have the same charm as the country burns she had known as a child in Scotland, but still they gave something of the same sense of coolness and peace that only water can give to a landscape, artificial or not. And it was instinctive when she eventually stopped beside one of them and leaned against a tree, so steeped in her own unhappiness that she was conscious of nothing else.

She had not even heard anyone approaching, and when Rosa Montañes' sharp voice addressed her she turned swiftly and looked at her with slightly dazed eyes. Mounted on Luis's gelding, she looked a formidable figure, and Kirstie guessed that Miguel's insistence on clearing her name had made the woman's dislike of her more virulent than ever.

It was too late to try and disguise the traces of those self-pitying tears she had shed, and the other woman made no attempt to conceal the satisfaction it gave her to notice them. 'You've been crying,' she said. 'Has someone upset you? Is that why you've decided to give yourself the morning off without saying anything to your employer?'

'I—I couldn't get in touch with him.'

Rosa's dark brows arched quizzically. 'Haven't you a telephone in that primitive little hut?' She laughed shortly, her eyes gleaming with malice. 'No, I suppose you haven't; it's all very basic, isn't it? Not what you're used to. Giving you that job was an act of charity on my father-in-law's part, of course, he can be foolishly soft-hearted at times. If he wasn't he'd have got rid of you long ago!'

Keeping a tight hold on herself, Kirstie gave her an answer that she doubted would get back to Enrique in the same form as she gave it. 'As it happens I'm giving up my job, *señora*, for—personal reasons.'

It sounded such a prim and conventional excuse and Rosa's sharp black eyes were watching her suspiciously, for she would suspect any unexpected move on Kirstie's part. Her dislike of her was almost paranoic. 'Personal reasons?'

Kirstie had no intention of giving her any more detailed explanation if she could help it, and she merely shrugged. 'That's right.'

'Something to do with your tattered Rodríguez pride, I suppose.' The probe dug deeper, determined to get at the reason for her sudden decision to leave her job, and Kirstie clung tightly to the pride she jeered at so mockingly. 'You didn't bother to tell your employer of your decision, obviously, or he wouldn't have been concerning himself with why you didn't arrive this morning.'

If Miguel had confided in no one else about her grandfather's proposition, Kirstie decided, he would have told his uncle, for they were very close, and she was suddenly overwhelmed once more by the memory of last evening's events. 'It's more than likely Miguel will have told him,' she said, her voice wavering slightly. 'He must know that I can't go on working there.'

'Miguel?' As usual the very mention of Miguel was enough to kindle fury in this explosively temperamental woman, and Kirstie noticed how her hands tightened on the rein, and her eyes narrowed. 'What has Miguel to do with you giving up your job? When did you see him?'

Kirstie had no special desire to cause further upheaval, so she chose her words carefully. 'He came to see my grandfather and me last evening, quite early,' she said.

'About business, of course!'

Kirstie flushed, resentment burning in her blue eyes for the implied mockery of her grandfather. 'Miguel *has* had some minor business going with my grandfather,' she told Rosa, 'but it wasn't to do with that that he came last night. It was something that Luis and I had planned, and Miguel had found out about it.'

'So he fired you!' There could be no mistaking the satisfaction that idea gave Rosa, but Kirstie wasn't going to let it continue.

Her cheeks flaming she stood her ground, looking up at Rosa Montañes with the same air of pride that distinguished her grandfather. 'No, *señora*, he did not! He came to let me know that he'd found out what Luis and I had planned and to put me firmly in my place, but he didn't fire me! However, since I'm leaving the Montañes' employ anyway, you have nothing more to worry about!'

'You insolent little bitch!' Fury blazed in Rosa's black eyes and Kirstie wondered how on earth anyone could be so quick to ignite; she was actually trembling with anger and the knuckles of the hands that gripped the rein showed bone-white. 'As far as you're concerned,' she grated harshly, 'I've *never* had anything to worry about!'

It seemed for a moment that Miguel's kiss burned again on her lips, and when she thought of what had followed, Kirstie forgot her resolve. She was unhappy and uncertain of what her future was going to be, and she hit out wildly at the woman who had always gone out of her way to make things as uncomfortable for her as possible.

'Yet when you saw Miguel kiss me first you were so furious you were even prepared to go to the length of having me charged with attempting to kill you,' she challenged. 'Heaven knows what you demanded in retaliation for that last time, in the stable, but as it happened I was forbidden to go near the stable again until you'd left. You should have gone ahead and called in the *guardia* when you wanted to, Señora Montañes, then you'd have been absolutely sure of having Miguel to yourself—or would you?'

Rosa cursed as Kirstie had never heard a woman curse, certainly not a well-bred Spanish woman. Kirstie recognised that she had perhaps been more malicious than she intended, but she told herself that she had cause to retaliate, and Rosa Montañes was more than able to hold her own. She had never intended either that this should blow up into a full-blooded quarrel, but it was too late to regret it now, for there was a look in the other woman's eyes that offered little hope of it cooling off.

Kirstie was no longer leaning against the tree, but standing beside the cool water of the channel in a tensely defensive attitude, not knowing what to expect next. Even so she could not have anticipated anything as coldbloodedly deliberate as what actually happened, and it took her completely by surprise.

Her black eyes glittering with fury, Rosa Montañes jabbed her heels into the gelding and rode him straight at Kirstie. A swift last-minute swerve avoided a ducking for horse and rider, but the gelding's shoulder thrust forcefully at Kirstie and knocked her off balance, while at the same time the heavy bone handle of the crop Rosa carried struck her a blow to the side of the head and knocked her backwards into the water. A searing pain in her head was the last thing she remembered; that and a very brief glimpse of her assailant riding like fury away from her.

She was in her own bedroom, Kirstie realised when she half-opened her eyes for a second, but there was a curious smell that she didn't recognise, and which made her wrinkle her nose even before she was fully aware of anything else. It was almost as if the very slight gesture was a signal, for someone moved beside the bed and someone else shifted at the foot of the bed, bending forward as if to peer at her, although as yet neither was identifiable.

'Abuelo?'

Instinct made her seek the reassurance of her grandfather's presence, and a hand on her forehead stroked gently as he leaned forward into her line of vision. 'Yes, child, I'm here.'

She turned her slightly uncertain gaze up to him and tried to focus on his face, frowning for a moment as she tried to recall how she came to be there; then she caught her breath and tried to turn her head in a gesture of denial. 'I—I was knocked out,' she began, but her grandfather soothed her gently.

'Don't try to talk, my dear, just stay quiet.'

'But she rode Suli straight at me,' Kirstie insisted, desperate for fear the vividness of the incident should fade before she told someone. 'And she—she hit me with her riding crop.'

'Rosa?'

The familiar voice from the foot of the bed brought a surging and almost choking violence to her heartbeat, and Kirstie turned and focussed her gaze on Miguel's darkly brooding face. How ironic that Rosa's action had brought him to her. His eyes had a deep, unfathomable look that defied definition, yet somehow there was an air of gentleness and concern about him that touched her as it always did.

'You!' she whispered, and her grandfather's hand pressed lightly into her shoulder, as if in warning.

'Would you like me to go?'

His voice was deep and soft, and he affected her even in the present situation when she was still not completely conscious. He was standing there at the foot of her bed and watching her in a way that would surely have sent Rosa Montañes into a fury of anger, and it seemed such a long time since she had seen anything other than passion or anger on those dark, arrogant features.

'You—you don't have to,' she whispered.

He looked at her for a moment, his expression defying

her need to recognise it, then he shook his head slowly and eased himself away from the tall, old-fashioned wooden bed-end. 'Nevertheless I think I will,' he decided. 'You should be lying there quietly not talking, and now that I know you've recovered consciousness there's nothing more I can do. I'll come back later when you're feeling stronger; if Don José will allow me to, of course.'

'Naturally,' her grandfather told him gravely. 'You're always welcome here, Don Miguel, and I cannot thank you enough for all you've done so far. I confess I'm not a practical man, and this kind of situation would have been beyond me; I'm very grateful for your help.'

Miguel heaved his broad shoulders carelessly and shook his head. 'If there's anything you need, please don't hesitate to call on us,' he told him. 'And I'll come later and hear the verdict, after the doctor's been.' He turned again and looked at Kirstie, a faint smile hovering at the corners of his mouth for a moment. '*Adios*, Kirstie, see that you stay quiet and rest.'

He was going, and something in her cried out for him to stay, although it made no kind of sense at all. It was just that his strong and vaguely brooding presence at the foot of her bed gave her a strange kind of comfort, and just before he reached the open doorway, followed by her grandfather, her still befuddled brain picked on something she had not really noticed at the time it was said.

'Miguel!'

Her voice was weak, but he turned swiftly, standing in the doorway with the sun in the little *salón* beyond outlining his broad shoulders and arrogant black head, and he held her uncertain gaze steadily. 'Haven't I said you should rest?' he asked softly, but she persisted.

'Listen to me, Miguel, please.' He didn't come back into the room, as if he would discourage her if he could, but it made no difference to Kirstie. 'Did you believe me? Did you believe me when I said that Rosa hit me, and——'

'This isn't the time for questions; you must rest.'

'But you said—Rosa, as if you guessed it was her.'

Her grandfather said nothing, she noticed hazily, as if he was quite prepared to leave everything in Miguel's hands, even in his own home, and Miguel was shaking his head. 'I've said I won't discuss anything until you're feeling strong,' he insisted firmly, 'and I mean it, Kirstie. Rest and recover and then we'll talk about it. *Adios*, Kirstie!'

He was gone, and the door closed firmly behind the two of them, and Kirstie sighed as she looked around the familiar bedroom. Her mind was still hazy and she felt very lazy, as if her limbs were reluctant to move. She was undressed, so someone must have done that for her, and also the smell she had noticed when she first recovered consciousness she now identified as a disinfectant of some kind, and when she put a hand to her throbbing head she found it was bandaged.

Obviously the accident, if one could call it an accident, could have been very much worse, and she wished her grandfather would come back so that she could question him. Her head ached and she felt rather sick, but there seemed to be nothing else wrong with her, except for that curious lethargy.

She could hear the hum of men's voices through in the *salón* and she was reminded of last evening, when she had stood and listened to the same two voices. If only she had realised then what it was that her grandfather was discussing with Miguel she would have interrupted them; and if she had had the faintest idea that Miguel was going to broach the subject to her she would never have gone out on to the *patio* with him.

Recalling the way he had kissed her, and what must have been in his mind at the time, she tightened her hands into fists and closed her eyes. So it was her grandfather found her when he came back, and he whispered her name anxiously, as if he suspected she had lost consciousness again.

'Kirstie?'

Opening her eyes, she smiled at him reassuringly. 'How did I get back here, Abuelo?'

'Don Miguel brought you.' He held her hand tightly, and something showed in his eyes for a moment that she had never seen there before. 'He came looking for you, because you didn't go to the office this morning, and when I told him you'd gone out walking he went to find you. I've never seen a man look as he did when he brought you back, soaking wet and unconscious, and for a moment I thought you might have——'

Remembering her black mood before she left the house, Kirstie reached up and clasped both his hands tightly, and her eyes shimmered with tears for the agony she had caused him. 'Did he say what happened?' she asked in a slightly unsteady voice, and her grandfather shook his head.

'He was in a curious frame of mind and he said little beyond the fact that he had found you lying in the water and that you had a bruise on your head. I don't think it had even occurred to him to call a doctor to the spot, he seemed to want to—' Don José shook his head slowly, as if Miguel's mood still puzzled him. 'He carried you into the house and laid you on your bed; only then did it seem to occur to him that you should see a doctor, and he went racing back to the house to call him. Only minutes later he drove back in the car with their housekeeper and she put you into bed and bound up your head. It all happened so—so quickly that I still can't quite believe it.'

How typical of Miguel, Kirstie thought, to have everything so speedily organised. Although his initial failure to call out the doctor was rather out of character, she had to admit, and she couldn't imagine what it was her grandfather meant about the curious mood he was in. It crossed her mind briefly as she lay there in that strangely lightheaded state of limbo, that Rosa Montañes wasn't going to like it at all, having Miguel running around after her.

She felt sleepy suddenly and her eyelids began to

droop, only the anxious enquiry of her grandfather
bringing her back from sleep for a moment. 'I think
can hear the doctor,' he told her, and for a moment sh
managed to keep her eyes open, but only for a momen

It had been several days, and the fact that Kirstie wa
beginning to feel restless suggested to her that she wa
sufficiently recovered to be allowed up for a while. He
grandfather was dubious about allowing her to mov
out of bed, but she was insistent. 'If I could just sit ou
for a little while,' she pleaded. 'It's no distance from
here to the *salón*, Abuelo, and I'd feel so much bette
sitting in a chair.'

'Perhaps so,' Don José allowed cautiously. 'But if yo
begin to feel drowsy or unwell, Kirstie, you mus
promise me that you'll go straight back into bed.'

'I promise!' She reached for her robe and was alread
tying it at the neck when someone rapped on the outsid
door. They both turned, and clearly her grandfather wa
uncertain whether he should stay and help her or g
and see who it was. 'Somebody had better see who it is
she told him with a smile, and as he went to do as sh
said she put a hand to the wild urgency of her hear
beat.

She knew that the housekeeper from Casa de Rodr
guez had been every day to keep the little *barraca* clea
and to cook her grandfather his meals, but Miguel ha
called too and something about that knock did not sug
gest it had a woman's hand behind it. The fact that h
hadn't once been in to see her was something that sh
had found herself resenting, however often she told he
self that he was simply obeying the doctor's instructio
that she was to rest undisturbed.

She was already standing in the doorway of her bed
room when her grandfather opened the door, and sh
listened with bated breath for the sound of the familia
voice. She wanted it to be Miguel, although her com
mon sense told her that now she was feeling almos
normal again, it wasn't going to be any easier to forge

he embarrassing position her grandfather had put her
nto than it had been before.

'*Señor*, I hope you'll forgive the intrusion.' The voice
vas familiar, but it wasn't Miguel's, it was Luis's, and
s Kirstie made her way to a chair and sat down in it,
he could scarcely believe how disappointed she felt.
uis was at his most formal and polite, and he sounded
uite unlike the Luis she was accustomed to. 'I wonder
 you'll give these to Señorita Rodríguez,' he went on.
 don't suppose it's possible——'

He hesitated to ask to see her, and Kirstie guessed
nat her grandfather wasn't going to ease the way for
im. Luis did not stand as high in the old man's estima-
on as he had once done, and he no longer saw him as
prospective grandson-in-law.

'Luis,' she called, and sensed her grandfather's dis-
pproval. 'Please, Abuelo,' she begged, 'I haven't seen
nyone for days, couldn't Luis come in for just a few
inutes?'

There was little else he could do, however he dis-
pproved of him, and Don José admitted him to the
ny *salón* with stiff courtesy. He would be far more
oncerned about her state of undress, Kirstie realised
hen she noticed him frown at her light robe, than either
he or Luis, but he couldn't change his mind now. It
ent without saying that he would stay and chaperone
hem, and that wasn't going to suit Luis.

He was carrying a huge bunch of roses which he pre-
ented to her with a slight bow and a small secret smile
nat her grandfather was obviously not supposed to see.
For you,' he murmured, and as she took them from
im with her eyes downcast, Kirstie realised they had
ome from the gardens of Casa de Rodríguez.

Miguel had been to the cottage each day, but he'd
ever brought her roses and it somehow added to her
iscontent where he was concerned. In the event she
miled at Luis, although it didn't quite reach her eyes.
They're lovely, Luis, thank you.'

If they had been alone Kirstie knew he would have

demanded a kiss in payment for his bouquet, but Don José hovering at his elbow restricted his normally flamboyant manner. 'Will you take a glass of wine, Don Luis?'

The courtesies must be observed at all times, and the invitation was as formally polite as Luis's answer. He inclined his head solemnly, at the same time managing to catch Kirstie's eye, but she ignored the wink he gave her because not even to please Luis would she make a mockery of her grandfather's old-fashioned mannerisms.

'Kirstie cannot drink at the moment,' Don José explained as he handed Luis his glass. 'Your very good health, *señor*.'

His presence definitely made Luis uneasy, but there was no way he could change the situation, so Luis must perforce put up with it. Glancing every now and then from the corner of his eye made him appear oddly shifty and Kirstie wondered what exactly he had on his mind and, more to the point, why he hadn't been before.

'I'd like to have come to see you before now,' he told her, almost as if he sensed her question, but Jon José interposed quietly before he could go on.

'It wasn't really necessary, Don Luis, when Don Miguel has been here each day to ask after Kirstie.'

Quite clearly that was something Luis didn't like either, and his frown showed a certain petulance. 'That's the reason *I* couldn't come, *señor*. Miguel told me that Kirstie was too ill to see visitors and that in view of the fact that he had been in at the beginning, so to speak, he had more right to come than I had. I didn't agree with it, but it isn't easy to argue with Miguel.'

'I imagine not,' Don José remarked blandly, and Luis frowned.

His style was definitely being cramped by having her grandfather there, and Luis liked things to go his way. 'Fortunately this morning I've managed to get here without him knowing,' he said, pointedly satisfied. 'And I know how you like roses, Kirstie.'

Unable to deny it, Kirstie smiled, but it was his company she was more grateful for, she had felt so cut off these past days, especially since becoming more conscious of what was going on. 'I'm glad to see someone to talk to,' she told Luis. 'For one thing, I'm dying to know what's been said about—what happened to me. I'm sure Miguel knew something, but he wouldn't talk about it that first day and I haven't seen him since.'

Again Luis gave her grandfather that slightly uneasy sideways glance, as if he would like to have said whatever he had to say without his overhearing. 'All I know for sure is that Rosa has packed up and gone,' he said, and Kirstie caught her breath, looking up quickly and frowning.

'She's gone?'

Luis spread his expressive hands and shrugged. 'She's gone. She went the day after this happened, and I don't think she and Miguel parted very amicably as far as I could judge. He drove her to the station, and the look on his face would have discouraged a harder nut than Rosa.'

A half-forgotten threat stirred in the back of Kirstie's mind and she looked at Luis anxiously. 'Luis, you don't think she'll keep Margarita from seeing her grandfather—because of this, do you?'

'I don't know.' His shrug suggested he had heard nothing of the threat to deprive Enrique of his granddaughter. 'I've never seen Rosa quite so subdued, as a matter of fact, even though she suggested a smouldering volcano waiting to erupt. Somebody, and I can only guess it must have been Miguel, must have laid down the law to her, because obviously——'

He broke off suddenly, and Kirstie's heart began a wild, fluttering beat as she too caught the sound of booted feet coming quickly across the *patio*, for this time there could be no mistaking who the caller was. Her hands clasped tightly together, she watched her grandfather move to open the door, before Miguel had time to knock on it, and this time, she noticed, he did not hesitate to invite the caller in.

Miguel loomed for a moment in the doorway, his tall figure outlined by the harsh sunlight outside like a figure of vengeance, pausing for a second when he saw that his brother was there. Then his eyes switched to the bouquet of roses that lay on the table beside her, and Kirstie saw his black brows drawn very briefly into a frown.

'Don José.' He greeted her grandfather with the deference he always accorded him, then came across to where Kirstie sat, and stood for a moment looking down at her still pale face and heavy-fringed, downcast eyes. 'Kirstie,' he said, so softly that the colour flew into her face. 'I see you're much better.' He spared Luis only a very brief glance. 'Well enough to receive visitors, it seems.'

'I dropped in for a few moments, that's all,' Luis told him, and Kirstie frowned because he saw fit to excuse his presence when she saw no reason for him to.

'And you're very welcome,' she assured him before Miguel could pass any comment. 'I'm very glad to see someone after lying in bed for days with only myself for company.' She reached and picked up the flowers from the table, holding the deep yellow roses to her cheek for a moment. 'And the roses are beautiful, you're very thoughtful, Luis, no one else brought me flowers.'

He took the allusion, Kirstie had no doubt, but instead of showing annoyance she could have sworn that his mouth twitched just slightly at one corner and his colour deepened. How dared he laugh at her for being pleased with Luis's flowers? 'Luis is of a romantic turn of mind, as I told you before he came,' he remarked, but for a moment when Kirstie met his eyes she felt certain it was resentment she saw there, not amusement.

'And didn't I tell you that I liked romantics?' she countered swiftly.

Luis's visit wasn't going as he had planned at all. He had anticipated sitting beside her bed and perhaps holding her hand, murmuring the kind of things that any girl would find conducive to getting well. Instead he had

een chaperoned from the moment he set foot inside
he door, first by her grandfather, and now by Miguel
s well.

His good-looking face had a definitely sulky look as
ne got to his feet, and he reached down to take one of
her hands, holding it in his while he looked down at her
with soulfully appealing eyes. 'I was hoping to see you
alone for a few minutes,' he told her, 'but—' He
shrugged eloquent shoulders and glared at his brother
before raising her hand to his lips. 'Perhaps later, my
pigeon, eh? *Adios*, my lovely.'

Kirstie would normally have taken Luis's extrava-
gances in her stride, but the present situation deprived
her of her usual aplomb, and she nodded her head and
murmured a rather subdued '*Adios*!' It wasn't easy to
behave normally with her grandfather and, worst of all,
Miguel standing by and watching every move.

He gave Don José a very brief and formal bow, but
ignored his brother altogether, then departed with all
the drama his extravagant nature was capable of. For a
moment after he had gone it seemed as if those remain-
ing were waiting for something to happen, and eventually it was Miguel who broke the silence as he accepted
her grandfather's silent invitation to take the chair his
brother had just vacated.

His proximity affected Kirstie as it always did, and
she wished she could conquer the sensation just for once
that made her feel as if her will was completely subject
to his. There was a suggestion of power in his broad
shoulders and bare brown arms, and it was much too
easy to recall how they had held her on more than one
occasion, so hard that she could scarcely breathe. And
that firm, straight lower lip was disturbingly sensual
when it was pursed slightly, as now.

'Are you really fit to be out of bed and receiving visitors?' he asked, and Kirstie couldn't help noticing that
her grandfather took no offence at all at his questioning
her.

'Don't I look fit?' she asked, but immediately regretted inviting closer inspection, because it was still more disturbing.

Black-fringed, heavy-lidded eyes moved slowly over every feature then came to rest on her mouth, and her pulse responded like a wild thing to the burning intensity of his gaze. His voice, when he answered her had the deep and breathtaking sensuality that she had heard on other occasions, and she wondered how her grandfather could not notice that at least. She wondered too what he would say and do if he knew just how much more vulnerable she was with Miguel in a romantic situation than she was with Luis.

'You look pale and heavy-eyed,' was his eventual verdict on her appearance, and such stunningly unflattering honesty coming after that explicit scrutiny took her breath away.

She flushed warmly and her blue eyes sparkled with resentment as she flung back the hair from around her face and looked at him down her nose. 'You're not very flattering, or very good for my morale,' she informed him in a small and shiveringly angry voice. 'Luis was *much* better for me, and you more or less sent him away!'

'Would you rather I went too?'

It was a direct challenge; soft-voiced and stunningly affecting, but a challenge for all that, and Kirstie guessed Miguel wasn't in the least surprised when she shook her head. 'You interrupted Luis when he was telling me about Rosa—Señora Montañes leaving, so you can tell me instead.'

She sensed her grandfather's frown, and knew he considered she had been too pert, but it was more difficult to judge Miguel's reaction. There was a look in his eyes that she judged to be anger, yet it aroused a curious feeling in her that she did not begin to understand. 'I drove her to the station myself the morning after you were hurt,' he said.

'Why?'

Her grandfather drew a breath to object, but Miguel

forestalled him, though she thought her asking came as a surprise. 'Why did she leave? Because I—no, *we* thought it the best solution.'

Kirstie stuck firmly to the path she had chosen and her eyes challenged him unmistakably. 'Even though you know she was responsible for what happened to me?' It was hard not to look appealing when she thought about how her grandfather had said he carried her home in his arms, and the strange mood he was in. 'You wouldn't talk about it when it first happened,' she reminded him, 'but I was almost certain you believed me.'

'I believed you—I saw it happen.'

His quiet matter-of-factness stunned her for a moment, and she stared at him, for she couldn't believe he had deliberately put Rosa Montañes out of harm's way, knowing her guilty of the attack. 'You—you saw what happened?' He nodded abruptly, and Kirstie's colour rose swiftly as she stared at him with shimmering blue eyes. 'You know what she did and you let her go home without—without doing *anything*!'

'That wasn't what I said,' Miguel corrected her quietly, and still her grandfather remained quietly in the background, Kirstie noticed bitterly. 'I can imagine how you must be thirsting for vengeance after the way Rosa treated you, Kirstie, but vengeance could only lead to more bitterness and too many people could be hurt.'

'*I* was hurt!' Kirstie reminded him, and her voice wavered slightly. 'You saw her hit me, but you simply let her go home as if it wasn't worth making a fuss about! I suppose to you it was more important to keep your precious name intact! No scandal to be attached to the Montañes name, and the Rodríguez hardly count for anything now, do they?'

'Now you're starting to talk that same silly nonsense again,' Miguel told her, and the cool, deep voice almost shattered her self-control.

'Don't talk down to me, Miguel! I'm not a five-year-old!'

Her grandfather moved forward, and she gave a sob

of exasperation when she saw him draw back again because Miguel indicated with a brief nod that he was capable of dealing with the situation. Getting up out of his chair, he came and crouched down in front of her, taking her hands in his and affecting not to notice her first ineffectual efforts to escape him.

'I think we'd better leave explanations until another time,' he said. 'You're obviously tired and still not up to talking for too long. Suppose you go back to bed and rest, and I'll explain it all later, hmm?'

His gentleness, his understanding had always been something she found annoyingly disarming, but in this instance she felt reassured by it and in some way strengthened. 'I—I'm all right,' she insisted, and shook her head to try and clear the tears from her eyes. 'I want to hear about it, please; I—I think I'm entitled to hear about it.'

'And I agree,' said Miguel, still holding on to her hands. His big, powerful hands were remarkably gentle, she had noted it before, and she let her own relax slightly. 'If you're sure you feel up to it, I'll go on, but don't fly in a temper with me before you've heard what I have to say, O.K.?'

'I'll try.'

He sighed, as if it was as much as he could hope for, then let go her hands and sat back in his own chair again. 'Everything possible was done to avoid what could have been a very ugly incident with long reaching consequences. Rosa claims that the blow on your head with the handle of her crop *was* an accident, and I think I know Rosa well enough to recognise it as the truth. According to her she was carrying the crop the wrong way round and had forgotten it when she hit you; she intended striking you with the lash, which to me sounds more feasible.'

'She also rode Suli at me quite deliberately,' Kirstie reminded him, and he nodded.

'That was a stupid and dangerous thing to do, and Rosa is no longer in any doubt of it.'

Kirstie was in no doubt who had impressed it upon her either, and the way he had told the story she had to admit it could be the truth. And she recalled how certain Margarita had been that she had struck her mother with the stick she was carrying; it wouldn't do to make such a determined judgment herself if there was the slightest possibility of it being wrong. Then she remembered something else too, and looked across at Miguel anxiously.

'Will—will she be coming back?' she asked, and shook her head hastily when he obviously did not understand her asking. 'I mean, she won't keep Margarita away from her grandfather? She did threaten to once.'

Miguel leaned forward in his chair with his big hands clasped together in front of him and his elbows resting on his knees. 'She'll be coming back,' he told her quietly. 'It's the price of getting away with the attack on you.' When she looked up swiftly to make a protest, for the first time since she had known him she saw a look of appeal in those deep, dark eyes and found it irresistible. Her protest was never made, and he went on in the same quiet voice, 'I know you probably think that you've had less than justice, Kirstie, but I was thinking of Tío Enrique. I don't know how you heard of the threat she made, but I couldn't doubt she meant it when she made it to me and my uncle.'

'I didn't doubt it either.'

There was a glimpse of warmth in his eyes that brought faint colour to her cheeks, and she hastily lowered her glance as he went on. 'I can't prevent you taking Rosa to court, even now, but if you do she'll make certain that Margarita doesn't see her grandfather again, at least until the girl is old enough to choose for herself. Would you want that?'

'No. No, of course I wouldn't. I won't take any action against her.'

'I thought not.' Again that warmth gleamed from the depth of his eyes and seemed to reach out to her. 'And now that's an end of the subject for the moment,' he decided. 'You shouldn't be out of bed so long, and I think you should go back, hmm?'

It was only when she turned to speak to him that Kirstie realised her grandfather was no longer with them, and she felt the colour rush into her face, for the move was so blatantly obvious that she felt ashamed of it. The lull she had felt while Miguel was talking to her was banished and in its place was embarrassment at her grandfather's determined matchmaking.

She got to her feet and she was shaking like a leaf, her face flaming and her eyes carefully evasive as she stood for a moment clinging to the back of the chair she had been sitting in. Miguel was on his feet at once, and reaching out his hands to help her. 'Your grandfather seems to have left us,' he said, 'so you'd better let me help you.'

Quickly she snatched back out of reach. 'No, no, I can manage on my own, thank you!'

He let his hands drop, but he was frowning, she could sense it. 'Shall I call Don José?'

Kirstie laughed a little wildly and shook her head. 'After he's gone to the trouble of leaving us together?' she asked. 'Don't play into his hands, Miguel, I've no intention of doing so. It was bad enough when he was set on marrying me off to Luis, but now he's approached you——' She turned quickly, almost too quickly, for she had to cling tightly to the chair.

'You find the idea even more unpalatable,' Miguel suggested, and there was a certain roughness in his voice that touched her senses. 'I quite understand, Kirstie— you can't imagine a worse fate!'

Had she really made it sound like that? Kirstie wondered. She stood holding on to the chair and needed its support, for her legs felt incredibly weak and unsteady. 'I—I didn't want to sound—ungracious,' she tried to explain, 'but you know how I feel, Miguel.'

'I only wish I did,' he told her quietly, and she turned again to make her way back to her room, and again he automatically reached out to help her. 'You're very unsteady and you need support, let me help you.'

'*No!*'

Shaking her head insistently, Kirstie clasped the robe to her throat and began slowly to cross the room, discarding even the assistance of the various items of furniture that she had used when she first left her room. But she had taken only one or two steps when she felt her legs begin to give way and she made a small anxious sound as she groped around her for something to hold on to. A week in bed had sapped her strength even more than she had realised.

'Kirstie!'

A strong arm was slipped around her and pulled her close against him, supporting her firmly so that she instinctively let herself go and clung to him, while the touch of him fired her senses as it always did. Miguel simply held her for the moment, his long fingers curved into the softness of her breast and spread over the span of waist and hip. Then he drew her closer still and his voice came from the region of her left ear.

'Now will you let me help you?' he murmured into the muffling softness of her hair. 'Or am I supposed to stand and watch you fall at my feet before you see sense?'

There was little else she could do but concede, Kirstie realised, and she nodded. 'I don't think I can get there on my own,' she confessed huskily. 'I feel horribly limp and my legs are so unsteady.'

'After a week in bed, my dear child, of course they're unsteady.' The whispering softness of his voice calling her his dear child aroused such a chaos of emotions that she protested automatically against it.

'I'm not a five-year-old, Miguel, and I dislike being called a child, I've told you before!'

For a moment the arm about her tightened so hard she felt as if her breathing had been stopped, but then he eased it a little and turned her to face him, putting the other hand around her cheek and lifting her chin so that she looked at him. His eyes, when she looked up at him in alarm suddenly, were deep and gleaming black as jet, and induced a shiver of anticipation that slid like ice along her spine.

'If *you* could decide which you are,' he murmured, his voice rough-edged, 'I'd know where I stand! You're child and woman in turn and neither seems to know her own mind!'

'I know,' Kirstie whispered defiantly, and flinched when a sudden harsh laugh startled her.

'Then you'd better tell me before I put you back into bed,' he told her, 'it could make all the difference!'

'Miguel!'

He ignored her protest and lifted her into his arms, carrying her through into her room, and as he laid her down on the bed Kirstie fought an almost irresistible desire to prove to him that she was a woman and not a child; definitely not a child. Instead she let her arms slide from around his neck and lay back on the pillows with her eyes downcast.

He said nothing, but stood over her, looking down with that steady disturbing gaze that did wild things to her pulse. Then he leaned over suddenly and touched his lips to her brow, a light, lingering touch that caught her breath. She looked up at him, her blue eyes between their thick black lashes almost slumbrous and her lips slightly parted because it was difficult to draw breath with him hovering so close.

Her head was no longer bandaged, but a faint mark on the skin showed where the wound had been, and Miguel touched it with his fingertips, brushing back the silky black hair from her brow. Kirstie could feel the urgent pulse that fluttered under his fingers and her eyes half-closed as if of their own volition as she instinctively lifted her face to him.

He touched her lips with his mouth, lightly and then much more firmly, though still not with that fierce passion she had known in him before, and her body arched upward as his hands slid around behind her and raised her from the bed. He drew her up until she pressed against the broad warmth of his chest and his hands were strong and irresistible as they held her.

She reached up her arms and clasped them around his neck, her fingers twined into the thick blackness of his hair. On those other occasions she had responded to his passion, revelling in its fierceness, and the lack of it on this occasion teased her senses so much that she sought a more fervent caress.

Instead, he released her mouth and held her for a moment, looking down into her face before lowering her back on to the bed. His hands slid slowly from behind her, light and caressing as they left the softness of her breast. 'We'll decide when you're better whether you're child or woman,' he said softly. 'For now you must rest.'

'Miguel——'

He quickly smothered her protest with a kiss, then straightened up slowly. 'Rest,' he insisted, and because his eyes had the glowing blackness of jet when they looked down at her, Kirstie made no reply. She watched him walk across to the door with lazy, heavy-lidded eyes, and there was a curious little smile on her mouth. Miguel turned in the doorway and looked back at her for a moment. 'And there'll be no more visits from Luis,' he declared firmly, giving her no time to object before he closed the door firmly behind him. Why Luis was not to be allowed to visit her again, she had no idea, but she was content at the moment to leave the decision to Miguel, and she closed her eyes, to rest as he said.

CHAPTER NINE

IT was just as Miguel had decreed, there were no more visits from Luis, although Miguel came himself almost daily. He treated her kindly and gently, but he had never once attempted to kiss her again, or even to mildly flirt with her. In fact he seemed to have forgotten those few minutes alone with her in her bedroom, and now that she was well again his attitude was beginning to irritate her. Just as it once had for quite a different reason.

He spent quite a lot of time with her grandfather and seemingly they talked business, so that Kirstie guessed that the business deal she had long suspected was between them was about to mature, whatever it was. Her suspicion was confirmed one morning, just after Miguel left, and her grandfather showed her a folder containing documents of some kind. The look on his face was enough to suggest that things had gone well, for she had not seen him look so pleased with himself for a long time.

'The first step,' he said in a voice so quiet she wondered if anyone else was supposed to hear, and she smiled at him curiously.

'What is it, Abuelo?'

Don José's eyes gleamed with pleasure and there was something very touching about the way he gazed at the folder in his hands, cradled as if it was something infinitely precious. 'Thanks to my good friend I now have shares in Casa de Rodríguez,' he said. 'I again own at least a small part of the Rodríguez estate, my dear child, and you cannot know what that means to me.'

'Oh, but I can!' Her eyes were misty as she looked at his face, and she blessed Miguel for bringing about something she had thought never to see again—a look of happiness in her grandfather's eyes. 'I know just how you feel,' she assured him, and hugged him tightly,

176

ressing a kiss on to his cheek. 'And I'm so happy for
ou, Abuelo.'

'It wouldn't have been possible without Don Miguel,'
er grandfather told her. He was gazing at the folder
gain and it was clear that he still had to convince him-
elf it had happened. 'I'm certain he let them go for less
han they're worth, but even so I had to sell everything
had left to buy them. Even some things that should
ventually have been yours, child, but I had to do it
nd—who knows—some day it might be possible to
cover them.'

'Abuela's jewellery?' she asked, knowing how he had
ung to them when everything else had to go, and he
odded.

'I'm sorry, child. Your grandmother wished them to
ome to you when you were twenty-one, but——'

'Don't worry!' How could she blame him when he
as so elated at being able to reclaim even a tiny por-
on of his ancestral estate? 'When everything is sorted
ut, we'll get them back, as you say.' She thought for a
oment, coping with a suspicion that lurked at the back
f her mind and refused to be dismissed. 'Abuelo, who
ought them? Who took Abuela's jewels?'

There was a certain satisfaction, a kind of challenge
the old man's eyes that confirmed her suspicion even
efore he said anything. 'Don Miguel paid me a very
ood price for them, child, and while they're in his hands
feel they're not completely lost to us.'

'Miguel!'

Her grandfather was too elated to even notice her
pression, and he closed the folder again with obvious
tisfaction. 'Just think,' he said, 'we have a little of
asa de Rodríguez back in our hands, doesn't that make
u happy, child?'

'Yes, of course it does, Abuelo.'

But there was one aspect of Casa de Rodríguez' future
at had not been mentioned lately, and Kirstie won-
red if he had taken it into consideration. It had caused
r a great deal of anguish when she heard the plan to

turn the house into a *paradore*, and she couldn't believe her grandfather would have wanted to be part of that.

Then she realised he was looking at her curiously and she smiled. 'Don't you regret acting so impulsively in giving up your job, Kirstie?' he asked, and she couldn't bring herself to deny it.

'Now that I'm better I'm beginning to miss going to work,' she admitted, 'but nothing's really changed. I still don't think I could face working with them all again after—well, after you and Miguel made me feel I've been—bargained for.'

'What nonsense!' her grandfather declared. 'You weren't embarrassed when he came here while you were ill, nor did you seem to find Don Luis an embarrassment.'

Kirstie had very mixed feelings regarding that particular visit, and she shrugged uneasily. 'Has Miguel said anything about his uncle getting a replacement secretary?'

'Not to me,' her grandfather assured her. 'As far as I know the post is still vacant, but if you're really interested in finding out, my dear, why don't you either ask Don Miguel when he comes again, or walk up to the house and see Señor Montañes? I'm quite certain he'd be pleased to see you.'

'I'm sure he would,' Kirstie agreed, far more tempted than she let him know. 'Señor Montañes is a very nice man, I like him.'

'Then go and see him. After all, you've never actually told him that you didn't intend going back, have you? You were hurt before you had the opportunity to let him know, so as far as that goes you're officially still working for him.'

It was such a temptation, but then when she took everything into consideration she didn't know what to do for certain. 'I suppose so,' she allowed, and Don José obviously sensed her weakening.

'Don't you owe it to him?' he insisted. 'It's only

ommon courtesy to give your employer notice, irstie.'

It was inevitable that she would go eventually, she uessed. There were too many things to tempt her back, ot least the sheer pleasure of walking into Casa de odríguez again and the familiar surroundings. She uld see Luis, and he was always good for her ego, dly in need of encouragement after more than a week Miguel's gentle aloofness. She liked Enrique and she d no doubt at all that he would be pleased to see her ;ain, especially as she had agreed not to complicate atters by taking his daughter-in-law to court.

'I could go,' she said, and Don José patted her hand provingly.

'But don't overdo things at first, child.'

Putting her arms around him, she hugged him tight. won't,' she promised. 'And I'm really thrilled about ur shares, Abuelo.'

'It should put an added spring in your step,' her andfather told her, and she smiled.

She saw no one until she came in off the *patio*, then e almost collided with Luis just leaving the house, and stared at her for a moment as if he could not believe s eyes. 'Kirstie!' He glanced quickly over his shoulder to the house, then took her arm and drew her back to the garden, keeping a hold on her as if he expected r to run away again. 'I'd begun to think you were ver coming back, and Miguel had laid down the law out me not coming to see you again.'

'And you didn't want to cross him!' Kirstie suggested th a half-mocking smile.

'Not on his own territory,' Luis said solemnly. 'But ver mind that now; how are you, my lovely?'

'I'm fine.'

'You didn't come to see me, I suppose? No, that's too uch to hope for, so it must be Tío Enrique.'

He didn't even consider Miguel as a possibility, she ticed, and wondered why Luis never seemed to realise st how much his brother could affect her. 'I did come

to see Señor Montañes,' she agreed. 'I thought I ough
to let him know that—well, that I haven't been able t
come for the last couple of weeks or so.'

'Well, he knows that, you divine idiot,' Luis laughed
'But I was under the impression that you'd given up th
job, Kirstie. Rosa said something about it.'

Kirstie would so much rather not have talked abou
it to Luis, but she seemed not to have much option an
she shrugged as casually as she could manage. 'I di
think about it at one time.'

'I wish I knew what it was all about,' Luis complained
'but all I get is odds and ends and I've never heard th
full story of what happened. I did gather that Rosa wa
responsible for you being hurt, so I took it that she wa
being stupid about Miguel again. *Was* that it? Did yo
fight with her again?'

Obviously when Miguel had said the matter was bein
kept very quiet, he had included his brother in thos
excluded from the full facts, so Kirstie was very war
when she answered him. Shrugging again with seemin
carelessness, she attempted to pass it off. 'Oh, it's a
over and done with now, and I'd rather not go into
again,' she told him.

'So you *did* fight over Miguel!' There was a hard an
very unromantic gleam in Luis's eyes, and she realise
just how jealous he was of his older brother's undeniab
sex-appeal. 'It's typical of Miguel not to take *yo*
situation into account when he wants to kiss you! If h
wants a thing he just helps himself to it, even if it doe
happen to be my girl!'

It wasn't the kind of conversation she had foresee
when she decided to come, and Kirstie wished she ha
encountered almost anyone but Luis. He seemed set o
talking about her encounter with Rosa, and its caus
and it was the last thing she wanted to talk about. 'N
one helps himself to me,' she told him, 'and I'm no
sure I like being referred to as a thing, Luis.'

'A figure of speech, that's all,' Luis insisted, and tha
sharp gleam was still there in his usually dreamy eye

Vhatever; I don't like him poaching on my territory,
nd I wish he'd stick to his own sort and leave my girl
one!'

Kirstie was feeling edgy and her decision to see En-
que and explain to him seemed less of a good idea
ery minute. Luis was making her irritable and his de-
rmined possessiveness grated on her nerves. 'I'm not
meone you own either, Luis,' she told him. 'I didn't
me with the property and the idea of *droit du seigneur*
long out of date! Neither you nor Miguel has any
ght to me!'

'Kirstie, darling!'

He was obviously puzzled, but Kirstie wasn't to be
rsuaded even by his practised sweet-talk, and she
shed away his hand. 'I have to go, Luis. I want to see
ur uncle and talk to him about—well, various things;
at's what I came for.'

'Not to see me?' Luis asked, and added as he nar-
wed his eyes. 'Or Miguel?'

'I saw Miguel not half an hour since at the cottage,'
e told him, 'and even you'll agree, I'm not likely to
ve followed him up here! I came to see Señor Mon-
ñes and it's time I went, or I may lose my nerve!'

'I'll see you again?'

It was rather more a demand than a plea, she realised,
d as she wasn't very sure just what was going to
ppen, she shook her head rather vaguely. 'I—I don't
ow, Luis—maybe.'

'I see!'

He looked at her for a long moment and his dark
es glittered with resentment for both her unwillingness
commit herself and her determined dismissal of him.
en he turned quickly and went stalking off along the
th to the stable with his dark head held high and
oking disturbingly like Miguel from the back. Kirstie
dn't know whether she was thankful or sorry that he
d decided to bring it to such an abrupt end, but she
dn't call him back.

When she knocked on the door of the office a few

moments later her heart was beating anxiously har
for she wasn't looking forward to the interview at
even though she did not believe Enrique would b
anything but kindly. It was because she felt sure b
knew exactly why Rosa had hit out as she had, an
she couldn't be sure what explanation Miguel ha
given him.

His smile when she walked in, however, banishe
most of her anxiety, and he did seem genuinely please
to see her. 'My dear *señorita*, I'm so glad to see yo
Are you feeling better?'

She took the chair he assigned her to and smile
'Much better, Señor Montañes, thank you.'

He nodded, looking thoughtful for a moment an
pulling at his bottom lip. 'I'd like to thank you for th
way you've behaved over this—this dreadful matte
Señorita Rodríguez. You had every right to demar
vengeance in the law courts, but instead you allowe
Rosa to go free so that I shouldn't suffer the loss of n
granddaughter. Miguel was so sure you would see th
reason of it, but—' he spread his hand in a touchir
gesture of doubt, 'I couldn't believe so young a woma
could be so understanding. Thank you.'

'Please—it was something I couldn't have faced, ye
losing touch with Margarita. I know how you love he

He nodded and for a moment his expression w
absent, then he leaned back in his chair and summone
his more usual smile. 'Well now, you've come to s:
that you'll stay on with Miguel, eh?'

Completely at a loss, Kirstie stared at him. Then sl
shook her head slowly and moistened her lips befo
she spoke. 'Stay on—with Miguel?'

Enrique looked at her for a moment, then clapped
hand to his forehead and moaned. 'Don't tell me—l
hasn't said anything to you about it? Forgive me, *señc
ita*, I quite thought that with all the time Miguel h
been spending at your home lately he would have to
you about our future plans.'

'Actually I haven't said a lot to him,' Kirstie told hir

d was quite unconscious of having pouted when she
id it. 'He mostly talks business to my grandfather;
's sold him some shares in Casa de Rodríguez, and I
n't tell you how thrilled Abuelo is to know that he
s even a tiny share of it back again.'

'Or how surprised _I_ was that Miguel decided to let
n have them! I can't quite understand why he hasn't
ked you about this other matter, though, unless—'
rique frowned and stroked his chin. 'He might per-
ps think you were reluctant to work for him after
ur remarks when you first came to see me, Señorita
dríguez.'

'Perhaps,' Kirstie agreed in a very small voice.

'Anyway,' Enrique went on, 'the situation is this, _seño-
a_; now that Casa de Rodríguez is paying its way,
iguel has decided that he can run it alone, so we're
oving back to Valencia to our head office, and he will
rry on here. I was under the impression that he was
ing to ask you to remain with him as his secretary, in
t I'm so certain he intends to that I have no hesitation
putting you in the picture.'

'He hasn't said a word,' said Kirstie, and her eyes
d a dark, thoughtful look for a moment. 'He hasn't
lly said very much to me at all in the past week or
days.'

'Then I can only hope he won't blame me too much
anticipating him.' He regarded her for a moment or
o, his hands steepled under his chin and a speculative
ok in his eyes. '_Will_ you stay on with him when he
s you to, my dear?'

Kirstie's thoughts were in chaos. She simply couldn't
agine not seeing Miguel every day, and presumably
visits to her grandfather would be less frequent now
t their business was concluded. 'It—it depends,' she
d, frowning unhappily. 'I couldn't bear to come here
e turned it into a _paradore_.'

Enrique looked as if her knowledge surprised him,
d he was shaking his head. 'You must have mis-
derstood whatever you heard about that,' he told her.

'The idea was never even seriously considered; Migu
wouldn't even consider such a thing.'

'Oh.' Kirstie wondered how many more surpris
were in store for her, and she flushed with sham
when she recalled how angrily she had berated Migu
for being the instigator of the idea. 'He—he vote
against it?'

'He simply didn't consider it, except as a joke,' E
rique assured her, and went on in a quiet, impressi
voice. 'I think you're under something of a misa
prehension here, my dear Señorita Rodríguez. Miguel
the senior partner in Montañes and Company, l
owns sixty per cent of the shares, and *all* of tl
Rodríguez investment. He bought out the rest of
very shortly after it got under way because he want
to branch out on his own. Although now it seems '
has let your grandfather in as an investor, albeit
minor one.'

Kirstie's head was spinning and she moistened h
lips with the tip of her tongue as she tried to come
terms with so many fresh ideas. 'I—I had no idea. WI
didn't he *tell* me I had it all wrong when I was so ang
with him?' she complained. 'He should have told me
was wrong.'

'I think,' Enrique observed dryly, 'that he was rath
hoping Luis would tell you himself, but I'm afraid l
faith was misplaced in that instance.'

She shook her head, still finding it hard to believ
'Luis?' He nodded, and Kirstie wondered bitterly if s
had ever before been so successfully made a fool of.

'He wouldn't risk turning you against him, of cours
Enrique observed. 'I told Miguel he wouldn't. Lu
should have been more honest with you and then ye
wouldn't have been so misled, my dear *señorita*. Ala
he sighed deeply, 'there seem to have been so many m
understandings, it's high time some of them were clear
up.'

Kirstie could only agree, but clearing up the thousar
and one things that had gone amiss between her an

Miguel would be a marathon task, and she had to confess she hadn't any idea where to start. Looking across the desk at Enrique's kind and speculative expression, she spread her hands appealingly.

'Where can I find Miguel?' she asked, and his uncle smiled.

'Not far away,' he said. 'You'll soon find him.'

Without a clue where to start looking for him, Kirstie automatically made her way round to the stable, but she hadn't quite reached the archway in the wall when he appeared. When he saw her he hesitated for just a second, then came striding on, while Kirstie stood and waited, her legs horribly unsteady, and her heart hammering away like a drum-beat that half deafened her.

That Moorish-dark skin showed like matt bronze against a white shirt and his long legs made nothing of the distance between them as he came across the *patio* to her. Kirstie looked up at him, speaking quickly before she lost her nerve.

'I have to apologise to you for—so many things, Miguel, but I didn't know, and you didn't say anything, not even when I was angry, and you could have put me right, you could have——'

His mouth stopped hers with infinite gentleness and he held her arms as he looked down into her flushed face and evasive eyes. 'Who have you been talking to?' he wanted to know, and she moistened her lips anxiously before she answered.

'To Señor Montañes.'

'And he thought I'd mentioned the business of you staying on as my secretary,' he guessed, and something in the way he said it made her look up quickly.

'He—he said you *were* going to ask me, but you haven't and——' Her eyes searched his face anxiously and the thud of her heart made it almost impossible to think clearly. 'Miguel, I didn't know you were against the idea of a *paradore*, you didn't tell me that it wasn't your idea, and Luis didn't tell me when I spoke to him about you.'

His hands moved lightly on her arms, stroking the soft skin and bringing an even more urgent beat to her pulse. 'I was rather hoping he'd tell you himself,' he said in the deep quiet voice that could wreak such havoc on her senses. 'But you were so determined that I was the villain that you probably wouldn't have believed him anyway, would you, my pigeon?'

It was the very first time he had addressed an endearment to her, and she was trembling, she realised, as if she was about to break down. 'I would have believed you,' she said in a shivery small voice.

His dark eyes scanned her face for a moment. 'Yes, I believe you would have,' he said.

He kissed her again, so lightly and gently that she longed to feel that fierce, hard pressure on her mouth again, and shivered at the recollection. 'I—I didn't know you were helping Abuelo to get back at least a small share of Casa de Rodríguez either,' she told him, and wondered how she resisted the temptation to lean towards him and make contact with the lean, passionate body that seemed to be taunting her with its nearness. 'I don't know how to thank you, Miguel, he's so—so happy about it.'

'I'd like you to know that selling me your grandmother's jewels was not my idea,' he said with a touch of dryness. 'So please don't blame me for it, I'd much rather not have taken them.'

'But Abuelo would never accept——'

She hesitated to say charity, but Miguel was shaking his head, as if he knew perfectly well what she had in mind. 'It would have been a loan only,' he insisted. 'I like your grandfather and I was prepared to advance him the small part he has and wait for profits to pay for it, for there will be good profits from Casa de Rodríguez, Kirstie, without resorting to tourism. But your grandfather is a proud man, and I respect that. As for your grandmother's jewellery, you need have no fears about that, it will still be yours when the time comes.'

'You think we'll be able to redeem it so soon?' she

asked, and felt a curious trickling sensation along her spine when he smiled.

'Take my word for it, little one,' he said softly. 'You shall have it when the time is right.'

Kirstie stirred in the infinitely gentle hold he had on her, wanting to respond as she always did, but inhibited by the constant reminder of her grandfather's matchmaking. Looking up at him, she shook her head despairingly. 'Oh, why did Abuelo have to have that silly idea of talking to you about—How can I feel at ease with you when you know what he has in mind?'

'I think we'll straighten out that question next,' said Miguel, and drew her into the shade of a magnificent oleander. His hands were tight about her arms and there was a gleaming blackness in his eyes that sent the familiar sensations shivering along her spine. 'First and foremost, the idea of my marrying you was mine, not Don José's, as I would have told you, if only you'd given me the opportunity.'

Kirstie was staring at him wide-eyed, and her mouth was partly open, her lips soft and rounded in disbelief. 'But——' she began, and Miguel once more silenced her with a kiss.

'Your grandfather complained about the way Luis was behaving and that was what made me so angry; that and the fact that you seemed not to be able to make up your own mind whether you objected to his behaviour or not.' His eyes burned between their thick lashes and she no longer looked away from them but met them steadily as if they hypnotised her. 'You seemed so often to be deliberately taunting me that I could have broken your lovely neck, because I was never sure enough of you to take a definite step and you were— you still are so very young. From the very beginning you got under my skin. Why do you think I let you have the run of the estate, and let you have the mare? I wanted you where I could see you, dote on you, and in the beginning you were so violently against me that I saw no chance of you ever changing.'

A flush warmed her cheeks and there was an incredibly yielding feeling in her legs as she stood not quite touching him. 'Abuelo always liked you,' she reminded him in a whisper, and Miguel took her face between his hands and breathed his words close to her lips.

'But I wasn't falling in love with your grandfather,' he told her softly, and the words stirred a wild exultation in her heart. 'I think my uncle thought I was losing my wits, I was so wrapped up in you, but he didn't laugh at me as he could so easily have done.'

'Laughed at you?'

She looked at him in sudden startlement, and Miguel shook his head, moving his thumbs lightly over her lips as he talked. 'You're not yet twenty-one, my lovely,' he reminded her, 'and at thirty-four I've had more than my share of loving. I took a chance in throwing you and Luis together, but somehow I knew in my heart that you weren't going to be swept off your feet by him, no matter if you did claim to prefer romantics.'

'I was never in love with Luis.'

She could say that because it was true, and she had never thought it was otherwise. She had come much closer to loving Miguel than ever she had to loving Luis, and she knew now that she would never love anyone as much as she did him. Miguel's black eyes gazed down hungrily at her mouth and she yearned for the feel of his arms about her and the touch of the strong, virile body with its demanding masculinity taking possession of her senses and her will-power.

He stroked her cheeks with his hands, then slid them down to her shoulders and pressed the long fingers into her flesh. 'I was wildly jealous of him, my darling, however often I assured myself you wouldn't fall in love with him.'

'You had no need to be—ever.'

Her voice was so light and husky that it was barely more than a whisper, and when he slid his arms around her and drew her close at last she lifted her arms to put

them around his neck. 'So often you've caused me to
doubt myself, my love,' Miguel murmured. 'When you
responded so warmly to my kiss that evening I came
down to the cottage, I thought you knew how I felt
about you; I was stunned when you turned away and
seemed so—disturbed because I'd tried to tell you I
wanted to marry you.'

'Because I thought Abuelo had talked you into it.'

'No one talked me into anything,' Miguel told her,
and his voice had the warning harshness of passion. 'I
asked Don José's permission to speak to you because
you were so young, that was all, although I met with no
opposition at all.'

Kirstie swept the black fringe of her lashes upward
and gazed at him with bright shimmering eyes. 'Ask *me*,'
she whispered, her mouth parted and half-smiling. 'I can
answer for myself, my love, I don't need anyone to speak
for me.'

Miguel folded his arms about her so hard it was
almost impossible to breathe, but she revelled in his
strength and looked up at him with her blue eyes
gleaming as brightly as his. 'I love you,' he whispered
hoarsely, and the hard virility of him fired her senses as
always. 'I love you, my little pigeon, and I want you
desperately! Marry me; in the name of all that's holy
say you'll marry me and put an end to this torture!'

It was like a cry of pain when he pleaded with her,
and Kirstie felt she had no resistance at all. She loved
him, and she had loved him for far longer than she realised; her need was as urgent as his and she parted her
lips in surrender, her words only a murmur against that
possessive mouth.

'I love you, I *want* to marry you—oh, so much I want
to marry you, my darling!'

His mouth was at her throat, her neck and fiercely
hard and passionate on her lips, every muscle of his
body straining her to him as if he wanted to make her
part of him, and if anyone could see them from the
house it didn't matter at all. Not at all.

Harlequin Plus

A WORD ABOUT THE AUTHOR

"When one happens to be an unmarried woman of forty-five and apparently fixed for the rest of her working life in a safe and settled job," Rebecca Stratton says of herself, "it is apt to be regarded as bordering on the insane to suddenly give it all up and become a full-time writer."

But that is precisely what British-born and -bred Rebecca did one August day in 1967. Writing had always been her ultimate aim, and she felt that if she didn't make the move right then and there she'd end her days as "one more elderly lady sitting and sighing for what might have been."

When Rebecca Stratton's first attempt at a romance novel was accepted, she didn't know whether to laugh or to cry. So she did both, and celebrated with friends and relatives. Then she sat down to the job of writing more books—and reveled in it!